PATRICIA REILLY GIFF

WILD GIRL

ALSO BY
PATRICIA REILLY GIFF

FOR MIDDLE-GRADE READERS

Storyteller
Eleven
Water Street
Willow Run
A House of Tailors
Maggie's Door
Pictures of Hollis Woods
All the Way Home
Nory Ryan's Song
Lily's Crossing
The Gift of the Pirate Queen
The Casey, Tracy & Company books

FOR YOUNGER READERS

The Kids of the Polk Street School books
The Friends and Amigos books
The Polka Dot Private Eye books
The Zigzag Kids books

WILD GIRL

PATRICIA REILLY GIFF

a yearling book

Text copyright © 2009 by Patricia Reilly Giff
Cover art copyright © 2009 by Eva Kolenko

All rights reserved. Published in the United States by Yearling, an imprint of Random House Children's Books, a division of Random House, Inc., New York. Originally published in hardcover in the United States by Wendy Lamb Books, an imprint of Random House Children's Books, a division of Random House, Inc., New York, in 2009.

Yearling and the jumping horse design are registered trademarks of Random House, Inc.

Visit us on the Web! www.randomhouse.com/kids

Educators and librarians, for a variety of teaching tools, visit us at www.randomhouse.com/teachers

Library of Congress Cataloging-in-Publication Data
Giff, Patricia Reilly.
Wild girl / Patricia Reilly Giff.
p. cm.
Summary: When twelve-year-old Lidie leaves Brazil to join her father and brother on a horse ranch in New York, she has a hard time adjusting to her changed circumstances, as does a new horse that has come to the ranch.
ISBN 978-0-375-83890-3 (hardcover) — ISBN 978-0-375-93890-0 (lib. bdg.) — ISBN 978-0-440-42177-1 (pbk.) — ISBN 978-0-375-89391-9 (ebook) [1. Horses--Fiction. 2. Homesickness--Fiction. 3. Family life--New York (State)--Fiction. 4. Immigrants--Fiction. 5. Brazilian Americans--Fiction. 6. New York (State)--Fiction.] I. Title.
PZ7.G3626Wh 2009
[Fic]--dc22
2008047733

Printed in the United States of America

10 9 8 7 6

First Yearling Edition 2011

**For Caitlin Patricia Giff,
beautiful Caitie, with love**

WILD GIRL

1

AIKEN, SOUTH CAROLINA

Sudden light burst against the foal's closed eyes. She needed to open them, and to get on her legs, which trembled under her. It was the only thing she knew, that struggle to stand.

And a feeling of warmth, the smell of warmth.

She opened her eyes and heaved herself up under that dark shape. Its head turned toward her, a soft muzzle, a nicker of sound.

Milk. Rich and hot.

She could see almost in a full circle. Another creature was nearby, its smell unpleasant, but she turned back to the mare.

When she was filled with milk, she leaned against the mare; she felt the swish of the mare's long tail against her face. She opened her mouth and felt the hair with her tongue.

Safe.

1

2

JALES, BRAZIL

My bedroom seemed bare without the horse pictures. Small holes from the thumbtacks zigzagged up and down the walls.

Tio Paulo would have a fit when he saw them.

Never mind Tio Paulo. I tucked the pictures carefully into my backpack. "You're going straight to America with me," I told them.

Everything was packed now, everything ready. I was more than ready, too, wearing stiff new jeans, a coral shirt—my favorite color—and a banana clip that held back my bundle of hair. My outfit had taken almost all the *dinheiro* I'd saved for my entire life.

"You look perfectly lovely," I said to myself in the mirror, then shook my head. "English, Lidie. Speak English." I

3

started over. "You look very—" What was that miserable word anyway? *Niece?*

Who could think with Tio Paulo downstairs in the kitchen, pacing back and forth, calling up every two minutes, "You're going to miss the plane!"

I took a last look around at the peach bedspread, the striped curtains Titia Luisa and I had made, the books on the shelf under the window. But I had no time to think about it; there was something I wanted to do before I left.

I rushed downstairs, tiptoeing along the hall, past Tio Paulo in the kitchen, and stepping over Gato, the calico cat who was dozing in the doorway.

Out back, the field was covered with thorny flowers the color of tea, and high grass that whipped against my legs as I ran. I was late. Too bad for Tio Paulo. He'd have to drive more than his usual ten miles an hour.

I whistled, and Cavalo, the farmer's bay horse, whinnied. He trotted toward me, then stopped, waiting. I climbed to the top of the fence and cupped my fingers around his silky brown ears before I threw myself on his back.

"Go." I pressed my heels into his broad sides and held on to his thick mane.

Last time.

We thundered down the cow path, stirring up dust. My banana clip came off, and my hair, let loose, was as thick as the forelocks on Cavalo's forehead.

We reached the blue house where we'd lived when Mamãe was alive. I didn't have to pull on Cavalo's mane; he knew enough to stop.

The four of us had been there together: Mamãe, my older

brother, Rafael; my father; and me. And it was almost as if Mamãe were still there in the high bed in her room, linking her thin fingers with mine. *The three of you will still belong together, Lidie, you'll make it a family.*

Shaking my head until my hair whipped into my face, I had held up my fingers: *There are four of us, Mamãe. Four.*

I remembered her faint smile. *Ai, only seven years old, but still you're just like your father, the Horseman.*

Just like Pai.

Two weeks later, Mamãe was gone, flown up to the clouds to watch over us from heaven, Titia Luisa said. And Pai and Rafael went off to America, leaving me with Titia Luisa and Tio Paulo. I still felt that flash of anger when I thought of their leaving without me.

I ran my fingers through Cavalo's mane. *I'm going now, Mamãe. Pai has begun to race horses at a farm in America, and there's room for me at last. Pai and Rafael have a house!*

"Goodbye, blue house." The sound of my voice was loud in my ears. "Goodbye, dear Mamãe."

Tio Paulo was outside in the truck now, blasting the horn for me.

"Pay no attention to him," I whispered to Cavalo.

Cavalo felt the pressure of my knees and my hands pulling gently on his mane, and turned.

We crossed the muddy *rio*, my feet raised away from the splashes of water, and climbed the slippery rocks, Cavalo's heels clanking against the stone.

In the distance, between his yelling and the horn blaring, Tio Paulo sounded desperate.

Suddenly I was feeling that desperation, too. We had to

go all the way to São Paulo to catch the plane. But I was determined. Five minutes, no more. "Hurry," I told Cavalo.

Up ahead was the curved white fence that surrounded the lemon grove. The overhanging branches were old and gnarled, the leaves a little dusty, and the lemons still green.

Pai, my father, had held me up the day he'd left. His hair was dark, his teeth straight and white. *"Pick a lemon for me, Lidie. I'll take it to America."*

I'd reached up and up and pulled at the largest lemon I could find.

"When I send for you, you'll bring me another," he'd said.

What else was in that memory? Their suitcases on the porch steps, and I was sobbing, begging, *"Take me, take me."*

He'd scooped me up, my face crushed against his shirt, and his voice was choked. *"This is the worst of all of it,"* he'd said. In back of him, Luisa was crying, and Tio banged his fist against the porch post.

But that was the last time I cried. After they left, I promised myself I'd never shed one more tear. Not for anyone. I told myself I didn't care whether Pai ever sent for me. I tried to ignore that voice inside my head that said how much I missed him, and how I longed to see my brother, Rafael.

Instead, I rode Cavalo all over the fields of Jales, I climbed out my window to sun myself on the sloping roof, I swam in the *rio* even though the water turned my fingers to ice.

Maybe that was why Tio Paulo told me a million times: "You may be small, Lidie, but how difficult you are."

"And tough as *ferro*," I'd say back, raising my chin high.

Titia Luisa would laugh, smoothing down my hair.

"You're not like iron, Lidie. You're like an orange, hard on the outside, but sweet inside."

Tio Paulo and I would look at each other, eyes narrowed; neither of us believed it.

Now I reached out, my fingers touching the dusty leaves of the tree. I could hear the horn blaring as I twisted off the nearest lemon and held it to my nose. Then I let Cavalo know with my knees that we had to race for home.

Cavalo took the fence easily, and we galloped back, the swish of the grass in my ears, a startled bird flying up.

I slid off Cavalo and put my arms around his warm neck, my face against his mane. "I'll miss you," I said. "Miss me, too."

I reached into my pocket for a peppermint. "I love you." I held it out, feeling his soft muzzle on the palm of my hand as he took it from me. Then I climbed the fence and ran toward the truck that would take me away from Jales.

3

TO JOHN F. KENNEDY
INTERNATIONAL AIRPORT

At the airport in São Paulo, Titia Luisa stayed in the truck, tears streaming down her face. "I can't bear to see you go, Lidie." She touched my hair, my shoulders, and I leaned against her for just a moment.

Tio Paulo was not in the mood for goodbyes. He hurried me inside, circling around knots of people. "A fine thing if you missed the plane."

"I'll just sit here and wait for the next one," I said as we stood at the end of an endless line. I waved my hand. "You don't have to stay."

"You'd be safe." He tried not to grin. "Who'd want to kidnap you, anyway?"

"They'd be happy to have me," I said, and was horrified to hear how much I sounded like him.

We checked in, then listened to an announcement that said the plane was delayed for an hour. Tio was in a fit of a mood now, and so was I.

We sank into the last two seats against the airport window. "You see," I said, "we didn't have to have hysterics, and rush like crazy after all."

Tio Paulo snorted. "You remind me of your father." He pulled at his mustache.

I narrowed my eyes. "You remind me of Cavalo when he has a burr in his foot."

We were sandpaper against sandpaper.

"You . . . ," he began, and then we both couldn't help laughing.

"I'll miss you after all," he said gruffly.

"Me too." My voice was so low, I wondered if he'd heard me. We were silent for a while. Then Tio spoke. "Do you want to know how your father became a citizen of New York?" he asked. "The customs people at the airport thought he might have false papers. They put him into prison until the next day."

My eyes widened in spite of myself. "They thought he was a criminal?"

Tio's fingers began again, smoothing his mustache. "No, no. The papers were real. Everyone apologized. It was fine."

Suddenly my flight was announced. We hugged awkwardly before he handed me over to the flight attendant who would take me through security. Just before I turned the corner, I looked back at him over my shoulder. He was still standing there, his hand half raised. I gave him a quick wave.

On the plane, I waited to see what it would feel like to fly.

In no time, the ground was speeding by below me: brown earth, spikes of grass, a crane spreading its pale wings. The trees became a smudge of green . . .

And I was in the air.

A dizzy tilt, a turn, and the white buildings of São Paulo were far underneath me, coming in and out of the mist. Then the buildings were gone, lost somewhere below. And so was all of Brazil.

But for one second, I saw a sweep of blue. Was it the ocean? "*Ai*," Tio Paulo had said once, "the waves, crashing together, rolling over everything, like you, Lidie, never still. You'll love the ocean."

I smiled to myself, even as my hands gripped the armrests: the plane soared up, reaching the clouds, and bounced through them. I swallowed. I was really on my way to America.

I settled back to practice my English, turning the pages of the little book Mrs. Figueiredo, my teacher, had given me. "Hello, hi, the weather is *niece*; watch out, the mosquito bites."

And especially, I intended to say to Pai, the Horseman, and my eighteen-year-old brother, Rafael: *I am hippy to be here*. I'd say it so they'd admire my English way of speaking; I'd say it so they'd be really sorry they hadn't sent for me sooner.

I kept practicing those words until I thought they were perfect as the sound of the plane's engines roared in my ears and the food cart rattled down the aisle, once, and then again. By this time I was tired and messy, my shirt stained from the extra food the flight attendant kept giving me. The trip was taking forever, but still I wanted to raise my hand and say *Not so fast*.

I drifted off to sleep, thinking about the moment Pai and Rafael would come toward me. *Hello, hi, I'm hippy* . . .

At last the darkness gave way to a million tiny lights, and New York was spread out before us. Somewhere tucked in among all those twinkling lights were the John F. Kennedy Airport, and the Horseman waiting for me.

Horseman, Mamãe's name for him. I could almost hear the sound of her voice. I pictured her in the kitchen when she was still well, her thick, dark braid bouncing over her shoulder, talking about horses with him, always horses. She'd say how wonderful he was with them, and that someday he'd be a great trainer.

After he'd gone, I learned about horses, too. I read dozens of library books, memorizing stories about Rags to Riches, the first filly to win the Belmont Stakes since 1905; Ruffian, who was called the queen of the fillies; Whirlaway, the great chestnut who won the three races of the Triple Crown. I listened to the endless stories Tio Paulo told me as he sat on the front porch. *I was a great jockey when I was young*, he would say. *Rode the best of them*. He'd lean forward. *I had no fear*.

His eyes would slide away from mine. I knew what he was thinking. I had no fear, either. But neither one of us wanted to be one bit like the other.

The plane was descending. From the small window, I could see buildings, and highways with what looked like toy cars moving along. Could I even remember exactly what the Horseman looked like after five years? It was only his voice

I knew from the Sunday phone calls, every Sunday for all this time. And the cell phone suddenly vibrating when I least expected it. "Lidie, what are you doing?" A few words, and then he would be gone. When he came home one year, at Christmas, I was in bed with the flu and was too sick to pay much attention to him.

I thought of his going to America, spending the night in prison. And Rafael, too? How frightening! Suppose the customs people in the airport didn't like my passport? Suppose they wanted to send me to prison?

I flipped open the passport; my picture looked like a girl with enough hair to stuff a mattress, a girl with two front teeth that overlapped a little. It looked like a girl who might have a false passport. I hugged it to me. Not false. It was a real passport, after all.

The plane bumped to a terrible stop. I slipped the lemon from my pocket to the depths of my backpack and clutched my papers in my hand. Then the flight attendant was standing in the aisle, waiting for me, smiling.

I wanted to hold on to the armrest. *Let me stay here for a minute, for another endless hour,* I thought. But, of course, I couldn't do that. I followed the flight attendant into the huge airport, a place full of noise, with stairs and ramps and escalators curving from one floor to the next like a giant snail.

And lines of people!

Everyone zigzagged along toward a row of windows to present their passports. My heart beat faster, and my hands felt clammy. But the immigration man behind his window asked only a few questions.

I nodded to each one as if I understood perfectly well

13

what he was saying, and when he frowned, I changed the nod to a quick shake of the head.

Stamp, stamp, went his machine. I was so relieved I told him that the weather would be *niece* soon for growing corns.

He lifted his eyebrows. Maybe he didn't know about those words. Maybe he was new to English, too.

We stopped at one more window. I nodded, shook my head, and we were through.

"Let's find your father," the flight attendant told me. "What does he look like?"

I tried to think of what to tell her. "Dark hair."

She nodded.

"Straight teeth," I said, closing my lips over my own teeth.

I raised my shoulders; I could hardly breathe. And suddenly the Horseman's face was blurred in my mind. I had no idea what he looked like.

Then I saw him coming toward me. The blur was gone; he looked exactly the way I must have known he would, except that his hair was getting gray. And were there tears in his eyes?

I had a quick picture of him laughing with Mamãe in the kitchen; I saw him holding me up in the lemon grove. And for a moment, I forgot about how angry I was at being left in Jales to wait forever.

He reached out to me, but as I took a step forward, I dropped my purse; coins rolled across the floor, so our hug was over in a second as we bent to find everything.

I stood up and saw Rafael. He was eighteen, so grown-up now! He would ride his first race as a jockey soon. But when he began to smile, I saw that his teeth were almost like mine, and his bony face as well.

He crushed me in a hug until I had to catch my breath. And the English words I'd practiced flew straight out of my head.

All I could think of to say were words in our own language. But my tongue was glued to the roof of my mouth. I couldn't even get them out.

NEW YORK

I waved goodbye to the flight attendant to take up some time while I tried to remember what I might say in English to the Horseman, but he was holding out a thick red hooded jacket for me.

I shrugged into it as he wound a scarf around my neck: pink with rabbits prancing up and down.

Good grief, bunnies munching on baby carrots. I tried not to look embarrassed. But what would people think of me wearing a scarf meant for a three-year-old?

We spun through the revolving door and outside to a polar-bear cold. Even the ocean, which Tio Paulo had said was nearby, must be frozen like the Arctic.

My eyes began to tear from the wind in that strange world with cars blaring at each other. People rushed around, stepping on my feet, saying something that must have meant *sorry*.

"You're welcome," I said back, trying to be polite, ignoring Rafael, who laughed.

The Horseman herded us around the other travelers and across the street. Would I ever be warm again? I thought of the poor lemon shivering in my backpack; it should still be on its tree in the sun.

But soon we were inside the truck, where the heater blasted warmth onto my frozen legs and numb fingers.

I kept stealing glances at the back of the Horseman's head, at this stranger I'd thought about all this time. He was leaning forward, both hands on the wheel, maneuvering his way in the traffic.

I looked at Rafael, next to him in front. Rafael turned toward me, grinning without saying a word.

Rafael, who had finished high school but on the phone said idiotic things like *How is your doll?* or *Do you still sing songs from* Snow White?

I closed my eyes, swaying a bit with the motion of the truck, and jumped as I heard the Horseman's voice again. "There's the most beautiful track in the world."

I craned my neck and caught a glimpse of stone pillars before the track disappeared behind us.

At that moment, I saw myself on the porch at Tio Paulo's, the library book in my hand, the sharp scent of geraniums around me, and Santos the dog chewing on a drooly old bone at my feet.

How many times had I paged through that thick book,

touching the pictures of that very race course, the great grandstand, the horse barns, the oval tracks?

I had seen the huge white pine tree, so beautiful that the track had been built around it long before I was born. And I had longed to be there.

Now the Horseman pointed to a school and, a few blocks later, a row of stores. We turned a corner, and then another; we drove along a road lined with bare trees and evergreens, then turned into a long driveway, the tires grating against the gravel. "Here's the farm," Pai said.

We passed a large house, shadowy in the darkness. In back, lights beamed down on a barn and an exercise track.

"I train all the horses for Mrs. Januário," he said. "She has seven, and we have—"

Rafael laughed. "One and almost two more."

I was too tired to ask what he meant. But then I saw a small house with light streaming from the windows.

"It's waiting for you." Pai smiled at me. "Home."

I stumbled out of the truck behind them and scurried up the front path in the freezing cold. We dived through the front door into a room that was truly warm.

The living room looked almost like Titia Luisa's, with pale yellow walls, but the green couch and the chairs were lined up in a row, reminding me of the dentist's waiting room in Jales. Terrible.

In the kitchen, a cake was on the table, with pink flowers and welcome words swirled across the top: *Bem-Vindo*. "I remembered you liked pink," Rafael said.

I hadn't had anything in pink for years: an insipid color, as Mrs. Figueiredo, my teacher, would say.

I sat there trying to smile around a huge bite of cake with the strawberry taste sweet in my mouth, but I could hardly keep my eyes open.

Pai waved his hand. "And in the hall," he said, "is the computer. Use it whenever you wish."

At last we went upstairs, passing a large painting of a jockey on his horse. Pai ran his fingers over the frame as we went by. I was too tired to do more than glance at it.

At the end of the hall, Pai opened a door. "Here's your room."

I looked around and gulped. It was a bedroom meant for a little girl. Snow White and the Seven Dwarfs had been painted on one wall, and reflecting them on the other side was a mirror with a pink bow.

They stood in the doorway, waiting. "We painted." The Horseman waved his hand.

I tried to smile, but I could see my face in the mirror. It looked as if I'd just had a tooth pulled.

Rafael pointed to the floor. In front of the bed was a small rug with the face of Minnie Mouse in the center.

"*Boa*," I said at last.

They both smiled, nodding at each other, pleased with themselves.

Ai!

"Rafael's idea," the Horseman said, and then they were gone.

I sank down on the edge of the bed, so tired I could hardly yank off my sandals.

But I made myself go downstairs to the computer. I e-mailed Titia Luisa: *XOXO*, and Tio Paulo: *So I'm alive*. Then I went up to bed and pulled the quilt over me.

I lay there, feeling numb; it was all so different from what I'd expected.

All strange.

I shook my head. What had I expected anyway?

Don't think about Jales, or the Horseman, or Rafael, who's so proud of his Minnie Mouse rug, I told myself.

I closed my eyes.

5

AIKEN, SOUTH CAROLINA

She was no longer a foal, drinking her mother's milk. She was a filly now. Her coat was a mixture of black and white hairs, and underneath, her skin was a gleaming black from a forebear of hundreds of years ago, an Arabian whose dark skin protected him from the desert sun.

The filly spent her days in the warmth of the field with its sweet-smelling grass.

She wasn't alone. The mare was there, and a bay colt and a roan, too. She waited as they began to run, standing still as if she were rooted to the earth until they were halfway across the field.

She chased them; the wind flattened her ears and raised her mane. She ran like the swift birds that flew over her head, or lightning when it flashed across the sky. She stretched her neck,

23

stretched her nose, stretched her legs; she reached the gate at the end of the field before they came near her.

A lake ran along the side of the field, and sometimes she drank, or cooled her legs in the shallow water. She always jumped back, surprised, when a small creature plopped under the surface, or a shell-like creature moved slowly along the mud away from her.

She never stopped watching, though, to be sure the mare was resting in the center of the field with one of the other mares, their necks crossed. And sometimes she went back to stand with the mare, or to feel the swish of that long tail in her face.

The one fearful part of her life was the two-legged one. He wore something to cover his small head, and a few times he had pulled it off and hit her flank with it.

He sucked on pieces of hay with his mouth, and when he made sounds with that mouth, they were loud and grated on her ears. With him was a small but fearsome creature with four legs; it raised its sharp claws when the filly came near and hissed at her.

The filly tried to stay away, but they were always there.

6

THE FARM

The bedroom windows rattled against their frames, and a poor tree branch, naked without its leaves, tapped lightly against one of the panes.

I lay there listening to the soft clank of the radiator bringing up the heat. But how quiet this house was.

In our kitchen in Jales, Titia Luisa would be singing as she prepared our rice and beans. On the porch, Tio Paulo would be clucking over the news in the papers, the pages he'd finished drifting down the steps. And outside, Santos the dog would be barking as he chased animals he could never catch. The only quiet one was Gato the cat, up on my bed, staring down into my face, while Maria the canary . . .

I padded over to the closet and reached into my backpack, first touching the lemon, then pulling out my horse pictures and the box full of thumbtacks I'd thrown in at the last minute. Who knew whether they'd have tacks in America?

Standing on the bed, I covered Snow White and the dwarfs. With my shoe, trying not to make too much noise, I hammered up some of my pictures: Native Dancer; Gallorette; Man o' War, who was called Big Red, and Whirlaway, my favorite of them all.

I tried to tell myself this was like my home in Jales. But where was the sunlight that used to splash over the floor and make plaid patterns of light on the wall? Where was the noise of the dog, the canary, Titia Luisa singing, and Tio Paulo complaining?

I went to the window and leaned my head against the cold glass. I was facing the back, and I could see a wooden barn on one side, and beyond that a single oval track, where a rider exercised a chestnut horse.

A white fence stretched around all of it, and at the far end, an orange cat was perched on top washing one paw. She reminded me of Gato.

Someone was walking along the path, whistling, and the cat jumped off the fence and disappeared into the trees as he opened the barn doors.

Suddenly I was excited. In that barn were horses. Horses! And I was going to be part of this new world.

I spotted Pai leaning against the fence, looking up at the sky. I looked up, too. A pale swirl had appeared in the gray sky, something I'd never seen before.

Snow!

I hugged myself. Maybe it was time to bring the lemon to Pai.

I scooped up the jacket up from the floor. It had spent the night covering the face of Minnie Mouse. And then I held the lemon in my hands, feeling its smoothness, smelling its faint scent.

Yes, I'd bring it outside.

I remembered to close the bedroom door behind me. I'd never let them see what I'd done to their new baby-pink walls or to their mural.

I flew down the stairs, past the dentist-office living room with the fireplace that looked as if it had never been used.

I struggled with the lock and went out the side door in bare feet. The bushes along the fence were covered with white; they looked like old men with their heads bent.

Snow covered my hair. I pulled up the hood and twirled around, arms up, breathing in the cold smell of the air. I tried to catch the flakes with my tongue, then took a breath; my bare feet were freezing.

The Horseman turned; snow had coated his graying hair and the shoulders of his leather jacket. "Your first snow," he said. "Isn't it beautiful!"

Suddenly I was shy, wondering if I should give the lemon to him. But before I had a chance to reach into my pocket, he swept his arms around, first toward the barn, and then toward the track. "Lucky," he said. "We've been so lucky. All of this belongs to Mrs. Januário, but I'm training her horses."

He spread his hands wide. "I learn from them, how they like to run, how they race. Some are in a hurry to win, others like to come to the front at the last minute." He touched my shoulder. "We'll use their strengths and win race after race."

I heard the excitement in his voice. My own heart fluttered as I held the lemon out to him.

He looked surprised—no, puzzled. He took it, shaking his head. "From the kitchen?"

"It's from the lemon grove." I swallowed. "From Jales."

He turned it over in his hand. "Ah, yes, I remember the grove. It belonged to the farmer down the road, didn't it?"

I nodded. A pain began in my throat and grew until it filled my chest. I felt almost the same as the day he'd left.

When I send for you, you'll bring me another.

But he hadn't even remembered.

I took back the lemon as if I'd only wanted to show it to him, and buried it deep in my pocket. Then we watched the snow coming down, covering the roofs of the house and the barn. I raised one icy foot and then the other.

Pai pointed to the front. "Mrs. Januário lives in that big house," he said. "She's in the South for the winter, but now that spring is coming, she'll be back soon."

Spring!

My feet were turning blue.

I tried to think of something to say as I reached down to scoop up a bit of the snow.

He looked down. "Bare feet! You'll freeze, child." He took my hand and we ran across the yard to the house.

A faint acrid smell came from the narrow kitchen, where Rafael was flipping eggs in a pan. "I'm a great cook." He rolled his eyes at me.

When we sat down at the round table, I realized he was

joking. The eggs were rubbery, the beans were dry, the bacon almost black. Rafael's eyes were dancing. "I'm a jockey who will ride horses in the races. I'm not a cook. Besides, Pai and I take turns with the meals."

The Horseman laughed. "After breakfast, we'll take you outside, Lidie, and show you the horses and the barn—"

"And now that you're here," Rafael broke in, "we'll teach you how to ride. Don't worry, we'll find a gentle horse. You won't have to be afraid."

I felt a quick flash of anger. They didn't know me, not at all. They were thinking I was the seven-year-old they'd left behind. I swallowed over the burning in my throat, reaching into my pocket, curving my fingers around the lemon.

Tio Paulo had said once that I was born knowing how to ride. I thought of Cavalo and the rides we'd taken, bending my head against the overhanging tree branches, climbing the rocks. . . .

Oh, Cavalo.

I took a breath. They didn't know that. How could they?

"I can . . . ," I began, but Rafael was pushing his egg around his plate, and the Horseman's head was bent over his coffee. I closed my mouth again.

Under a leaden sky, we took the path with its deepening snow around the track to the barn. The roof was low, with icicles hanging along the edge. Rafael reached up, knocking two off, and handed one to me. "It's the taste of winter," he said.

The icicle was cold in my fingers, cold against my lips, reminding me of ice cubes that clinked in a soda glass on a summer day.

29

We went through the open doors into the barn, where a few chickens wandered around in the hay. Stalls lined both sides of the aisle, and horses looked out over half doors: three chestnuts, and a bay so dark his coat gleamed almost black. They were as curious to see me as I was to see them, their eyes wide under their long curving eyelashes.

I brushed my hand against one of the chestnuts, and reached down into a pail of carrots. I stood watching as the horse took the carrot and chewed with her thick yellow teeth.

A man with leathery skin sat on a stool in the aisle.

"José. That's me. I do everything around here." He laughed, his Portuguese thick on his tongue. "Well, a few things, anyway."

"Lidie," I said. "And that's me. I saw you carrying a pail before."

That reminded me. "Is the cat . . ." I hesitated before I said *ours*. The word seemed wrong; nothing here really belonged to me.

Pai lifted one shoulder. "The orange cat? A stray. He doesn't belong to anyone."

I swallowed. "Poor cat."

Pai's hand swept around the stalls. "Only one horse here is actually mine, but two more are coming. One who might race someday . . ." He paused. "And another . . ."

"Who won't." Rafael rolled his eyes. He beckoned to me, and we walked to the end stall. "Doce, our horse. Sweet like his name."

I raised my hand to touch his soft muzzle and to rub his chestnut forehead.

"I'll ride her in a few weeks," Rafael said. "And by that time, Lidie, you'll know how to ride, too."

I smiled, a secret smile. I pictured how it would be, how I'd surprise him.

Rafael would be on one horse and I on another. I might even hold back and let him get a head start. And then . . .

Then.

He'd see.

And so would the Horseman, who didn't remember the lemon.

Even Tio Paulo would be smiling if he knew about my plan.

AIKEN, SOUTH CAROLINA

During the night, the filly heard the sound of the bay whinnying, and the low grunts of the roan. She heard the creature, too, his footsteps outside her stall.

Next to her, the mare's ears were pricked forward, listening. The filly raised one hoof uneasily and moved behind the mare. She felt the swish of that long thick tail and nibbled at it.

After a while, she slept again.

In the morning, she and the mare were led out to the field. She looked for the roan and the bay, but they never came.

Later the creature moved along the outside of the fence. She watched as he opened the gate to the far field—the field with sweet grass and clover.

The creature was gone.

The filly moved slowly, taking her time. Even when she was within a few feet of the gate, she wasn't sure if she'd go through.

She glanced back at the mare, then took a step, and another, into the field with its wonderful smell of clover.

And behind her . . .

Behind her . . .

The gate slammed shut.

She ran along the fence, once, twice, back and forth, but there was no way out. And near her, on the fence, the small one raised its claws and hissed.

The filly whinnied, her voice high with panic. She was able to take one last look at the mare, that huge chestnut body with its swishing tail, the great dark eyes. The mare was trying to get to her, too, running back and forth on the other side of the fence, making frightful sounds.

But the creature was back, pushing her until she was inside a space like a stall—not her stall. She kicked out at him, but he jumped away.

She felt movement under her. The sound of her own voice was as terrible as the rumble of noise as the tiny stall bumped across the field and away.

She didn't stop her cries.

Not for a long time.

She was alone.

Then it was night again, and she slept.

8

WOODHILL SCHOOL

I awoke thinking I'd been here for more than a week. I angled my head to see the picture of Gallorette, the great tomboy mare, seventeen hands, bigger than many stallions. It was as if she were staring back at me with her dark eyes.

Next to her was Native Dancer, the gray ghost, with his lovely silver face. The blur in the corner of the photo was the stray black cat Native Dancer loved, and that traveled with him wherever he went.

I smiled at my pictures. Today was my first day of school.

I grabbed my clothes from the dresser. I'd packed them carefully, thinking of this day: a yellow top and jeans with small flowers to match.

I put the sandals back in the closet; what good would they be against the snow outside? It was a good thing the

Horseman had bought boots for me yesterday. He'd wanted to buy pink ones with cat faces in front, but how could I have worn them in sixth grade?

I'd pointed to striped boots and he'd frowned. I'd put out my chin, standing there silently, trying to look as if I didn't care, until he'd told the woman to wrap up the striped ones.

Today the early morning went by in a blur: I ate a quick breakfast of bread dipped in honey and coffee laced with milk as the Horseman and Rafael tried to stuff my head full of English.

I held up my hand. "I know English, what do you think?" I would never let them know how worried I was.

Rafael tilted his head. "I'll make you a terrific sandwich for lunch."

I watched as he put some kind of strange meat on two slabs of bread and filled the whole thing up with lettuce leaves. He smushed it together and dumped it into a bag with an apple.

"Nice, right?" he said in English. "A wonderful lunch."

Ah, *nice*, not *niece*.

As the Horseman and I pulled out of the driveway, I whispered some of my words: *tree, forest,* and *watch out, the mosquito bites,* and added a few new ones: *horse, barn, snow.* At supper every night, I had repeated sentences with Pai and Rafael, but they had disappeared somewhere into the back of my head. I had to hope the English words would come to me when I needed them.

We parked in front of a school built of faded red bricks. Next to the huge doors, an American flag blew in that cold wind. The metal clips that held it to the pole clanked, and withered leaves skittered across the snowy yard.

I shivered. It was so unlike the school at home with the windows opened wide to catch the breeze. The colors here were almost dull, as if the world were washed in gray paint.

I didn't want to go inside; it was . . . too much. But then I remembered what Titia Luisa had told me once: *You, Lidie, will learn everything there is to know. You'll do something wonderful with your life.*

And Mrs. Figueiredo, my teacher for the last two years, had said: *You are as smart as any child I've ever taught, Lidie.*

I held on to those two memories as the Horseman took me inside and kissed me goodbye. Then a teacher with a pencil in her pouf of hair walked me to a classroom. She talked the whole time, pointing at doors, at the long window at the end of the hall.

I nodded. "Yes, nice." Through that window I could see a tree, its branches gray against the sky. "Nice . . . ," I said again. "Nice tree."

I walked with my head up now. My words were turning out to be very useful.

The pencil teacher opened the classroom door, and another teacher came toward us. She patted my shoulder, talking slowly, introducing me to the class. I couldn't find a place to fit in any of my words except *hi*, and I was too shy to say it. I thought about *watch out, the mosquito bites*; it wouldn't work here in a million years.

Jackets hung along the side of the room. All of them had different colors, and for the first time, I saw that this place could be bright and cheerful. I unwound myself from my own jacket, glad that the bunny scarf was under my bed where no one would see it. In my head, I told the jacket, *You belong here now.*

A girl looked up, patting the seat next to her, and someone else reached out to pat my arm as I walked past to the empty seat at the table. Was that what they did in America, patted everyone who came into the room or walked by?

But the boy in front of me just leaned over and drummed with his fingers on the table. "Ian," he said, and smiled. "Hi, shrimp."

Shrimp?

What was that? It sounded like something lovely, so I smiled at him. "Hi, shrimp," I said, too, and he burst out laughing.

"Ian," the girl said with an edge to her voice.

He raised his shoulders and smiled at me.

"Okay," I said. What was going on?

The teacher clapped her hands once, and everyone stood suddenly and changed seats with a great clatter. The girl who had patted the empty seat pulled me along with her to a table near the window. "Liz." She pointed to herself.

How strange to have a name that sounded like a swarm of bees. I nodded as if I approved. "Lidie." I pointed to myself, glad my name sounded more like a flower.

Liz asked me questions, talking loudly as if I were deaf. She took books out of a drawer in the table, one for her and one for me. I spotted a picture with a lot of trees. Ah, yes. "Forest," I said.

She smiled and mumbled something that sounded like—was it *certo*? She spoke my language! I felt the relief of it in my throat and chest.

I let a flood of my own words come, telling her about Jales and coming here, and the most important thing: I had to go to the bathroom.

My talking wound down like Titia Luisa's old clock. Liz's eyes told me that she didn't understand a word. She raised her shoulders helplessly. I turned toward the teacher, who was standing still, looking at me. I saw something in her eyes, too; she felt sorry for me.

I felt sorry for myself. The morning took forever to move itself along. When everyone bent over their books, reading, all I could do was page through mine, pretending the silly trees were fascinating.

All the time, I thought about bathrooms: the one outside Mrs. Figueiredo's classroom, with the row of faucets that dripped; the one in the barn yesterday, with its wonderful drawing of Man o' War on the door: all the bones carefully marked, the muscles outlined.

At last I couldn't wait anymore. I took a deep breath and went up to the teacher. I patted her shoulder nicely and pointed to the door.

The teacher smiled and pointed to herself. "Mrs. Bogart."

I shook my head and moved toward the door. I'd have to run down the hall and open all the doors until—

Mrs. Bogart stepped in front of me. She took papers off her desk, then led me back to my seat, talking. She opened the blank notebook the Horseman had bought for me and smoothed down the first page with her large hands. Then she put her own papers next to it.

Baby math problems.

Mrs. Figueiredo's lip would have curled up at these. But there was no time to think of the math problems a six-year-old could easily solve. I felt the wetness coming, seeping into my lovely jeans with the yellow flowers. I sat there, frozen.

But the girl, Liz, next to me and the teacher finally realized what was happening. The teacher made a small sound, a sound you could tell, in any language, was sad, was sorry.

I crumpled up the math paper, hearing the sound of it as I threw it on the floor. I stood up with everyone turning to look at me.

I went to the side of the room and pulled my jacket off the hook. It didn't belong there.

With the teacher calling after me, I opened the door and looked for the nearest way out. Before she could catch up, I was outside in the cold, running.

9

NEW YORK

As I ran, I zipped my jacket up to my neck, feeling it rip into my skin. I heard the *clink clank* of the flagpole clips in the cold wind that took my breath away. My flowered jeans were stuck to my legs.

I turned the corner away from school. Behind me the teacher called, "Lidia!"

She didn't even know how to say my name. "Lidie," I yelled back over my shoulder, my voice mean and angry.

I didn't wait to see if she'd heard me. I turned into a new street. I'd never go back to that school, where everyone knew what had happened. I wouldn't grow up the way Titia Luisa said I would, doing something wonderful with my life. And someday, when Mrs. Figueiredo heard that I'd never gone to school, how disappointed she'd be.

But no one would be as disappointed as I was.

I reached a wide street with cars running back and forth, slush spraying from their wheels. Everything was in a hurry here, even the snow, which was melting with great drops coming from the bare tree branches, and water gurgling along the curb.

I didn't know where I was. I passed stores. One smelled of eggs cooking and some kind of meat, another had signs with words pasted all over the windows. Not my words—but I was never going to learn English, anyway.

Inside another store were piles of vegetables and fruit. I stopped to look at them. Pathetic. In Jales, the broccoli would be twice that size, rich and dark. In Jales, the pole beans would be plump, the cucumbers shiny green, and the grapes in thick purple bunches.

If only I were back in Titia Luisa's house, snapping beans into the colander or fighting with Tio Paulo over the last banana in the bowl. If only I had my cell phone.

But how could I call the Horseman? How terrible it would be to tell him what had happened.

But how could I not? How could I wander around in this cold, alone?

Make a plan, I told myself, trying to fight away the panic that was coming up from my chest to choke me.

Suppose I went into that fruit store and asked the owner to help me. What could I say, *nice*, *tree*, *farm*?

Yes. *Farm*.

I would say *farm*, and the store man might know I wanted to go there. He'd pick up the phone and call the Horseman. I tried not to think about that part.

So that was what I did. Pulling my jacket down as far as

I could so it almost reached my knees, I went into the store and placed myself in front of the counter.

I could see immediately that this man wasn't as friendly as he might be. I smiled and in my best English said, "Farm." At the last minute, I remembered to add "Please."

The man blinked.

I said my two words again, my hands gripping each other. The man shrugged, so I said it again.

His face was blank; he didn't even understand his own language. And now people were waiting in back of me.

I stepped away and went out the door. Anyone with such sickly vegetables was not a person I cared to talk to, anyway.

I looked back. The man was staring at me, and so were the two women in line. I turned the corner, suddenly afraid.

Somehow I'd be saved. Maybe the Horseman would come along in his truck, or there'd be someone walking by. But what would I say? What? I was so cold now, almost too cold to think.

Mrs. Figueiredo's face came into my head. It was almost as if she was smiling at me, her face tilted. I could even see the freckles on her cheeks.

If I were in Jales, I'd be sitting at my desk with the classroom window next to me, and outside I'd see the yellow hibiscus blooming. *You can do this, Lidie*, she had said a hundred times, about a math problem, an essay, a difficult page in my science book.

And what about Tio Paulo that time I had that huge splinter in my thumb? I'd gritted my teeth as he took it out with a needle, telling myself he could cut off my finger before I'd let him know how much it hurt.

He'd said, *You have the strength of ten.*

I had turned away so he wouldn't see how pleased I was.

So now I said aloud: "You can do this, Lidie. You have the strength of ten." And before I could lose my courage, I went back to the fruit store.

Another set of women stood in line with their poor vegetables in baskets. I reached across them for a pen on the counter and stood on tiptoes for a paper bag.

They watched as I drew the barn. I drew a horse going into the barn, relieved that the animal actually looked like a horse.

"*Ajuda,*" I said, and suddenly remembered the English word. "Help." And then like a light going off in my brain: "*Perdida.* Lost."

"Ah," they said, almost together. They gathered around me, and one of them patted my shoulder. Of course.

The man picked up the phone. At the same time, he opened a bottle of *suco de laranja* and poured the orange juice into a cup for me. I drank it with my back against the counter so no one could see what had happened to my flowered jeans.

I heard him say something that sounded like *policia.* I thought of my passport picture and the story Tio had told me about Pai in prison.

Would I be arrested? I thought about running. I put down the juice and took a step, but before I could move, two policemen unfolded themselves from a car outside. I looked toward the back of the store. Was there any way I could escape?

But the policemen smiled, talking to me so fast I wondered how they even understood themselves.

A few minutes later, Rafael came, almost dancing around a bin of pale lettuce, and reached out to me.

"How did you know where I was?" I leaned against him.

"Oh, Lidie, the school called. And we called the police. Everyone is out looking for you."

One of the policemen looked at me. "Okay now?"

"Okay." I waved my hand to show him he could leave.

I turned to Rafael. "I'm never going back to school." I said it with anger. Anger at this school. Anger at him. Anger that nothing was the way I had dreamed it back on Tio Paulo's porch.

Everyone was smiling at me. They wouldn't be smiling if they knew what I was saying, or worse, what I was thinking.

"School is good," Rafael said. "Why not?" He reached for his cell phone.

I shook my head. I certainly wasn't going to tell him about my flowered pants. "They don't know how to speak right," I said.

Rafael laughed, showing the one tooth that overlapped another. He spoke quickly into the phone, first in our language, telling the Horseman that I'd been found, and then something in English.

"Come on," he said. "Let's go."

I nodded to the man behind the counter, who had turned out to be friendlier than he looked. He came around and held out his hand. I shook his hand and waved back at the women until we were in the truck, driving away from there.

"Don't take me back to school," I said. "I'll only run away again."

"I wouldn't think of it," he said. "We're going someplace else." He sounded as if he were talking to a four-year-old.

I took a breath.

"Not home," he said.

"Home is Jales. Home is the lemon grove, and Mrs. Figueiredo, and—"

"We're not going there, either," he said. "We'd never get there in this old truck."

"I didn't ask you to joke," I said.

"*Ai*, Lidie." He turned to look at me. "Do you think I don't know how hard it is? When I came here, I cried every night for Mamãe and the house on the hill."

I could feel my eyes burning. "We're going to be in an accident if you don't keep your eyes on the road."

"I cried for you for a long time," he said. "My sweet baby sister."

I swallowed, feeling a lump in my throat. Crying for me? I couldn't remember anyone caring about me as much as that since Mamãe had died.

I wanted to say a hundred things to him, things like *I'm not a baby, Rafael, I haven't been a baby in a long time*; things like *I'm glad you cried for me*, things like *I still miss Mamãe, who used to dance us around in the living room.*

But I couldn't talk.

I thought about the Horseman, my running out of school, and the police coming. How could everything have gone so wrong so quickly?

Rafael said, "I'll tell you where we're going, Lidie. To the races."

10

NEAR HARRISBURG,
PENNSYLVANIA

Sometimes the van was still. It was then that the filly made the greatest noise, kicking, neighing, her ears pasted flat with grief and anger. But then the floor rumbled, and she began to sway with the movement again.

At last it stopped, and the noise, too. Everything was quiet.

She was hungry and thirsty. She pulled some of the dried grass from the hanging bag and took huge gulps of water from the pail.

Behind her, everything opened.

She turned her head to see the creatures standing there.

She kicked once. Kicked again.

One of them climbed in with her.

She reared up on her back legs, but the creature darted around her. The others pushed at her, and she was pulled outside . . .

To the air, to the cold.

And in one moment, there was an open space. She raised her head and ran.

The ground was wet underneath, but that didn't stop her.

She raced the way she had in the field with the others. Raced as fast as the birds flew overhead.

Raced across the field with the creatures far behind her.

She came to a stop at a fence that was too high to jump. She stood there, looking at the trees on the other side. There was no place to go.

The creatures caught up with her at last. She could hear the sound of their hard breathing. They pulled on her lead and took her to an empty stall . . .

Without the mare.

Alone.

11

THE TRACK

It had begun to rain, a cold, soaking rain, as Rafael drove between the great stone pillars and pulled into the track. We stumbled out, heads down; in a moment, my hair and jacket were soaked.

The huge white pine tree with dripping branches stood in front of the grandstand. I thought of all the champion horses that had pranced past that tree on their way to win.

I was standing where Whirlaway had walked, and Native Dancer, and Ruffian, who was buried at the racetrack, her nose pointing toward the finish line.

"Are you hungry?" Rafael asked.

I glanced back at the truck, but my lunch bag had disappeared. It might still be in the classroom for all I knew. I shrugged helplessly. "I don't know what happened to my lunch."

"Don't worry." He took my arm, and we went into the cafeteria. As we walked along the counter with our trays, I breathed in the smell of fried onions and hamburgers sizzling on the grill.

"You have to have a hot dog with mustard and sauerkraut and pickles, and some of those onions," Rafael said. "It's the best."

And that was what I had, with fruit juice, and a sticky Danish with a round of cheese in the center like a warm sun. I ate slowly, thinking about what would happen when we went home. What would I say to the Horseman? What would he say to me?

Rafael was having a hot dog, too, but he ate only half. He washed it down with a Diet Coke and threw the rest of it away.

"Very wasteful," I said. I sounded like Titia Luisa.

He raised his shoulders. "Worry about yourself," he said, but nicely. "Now, what pleases you, Lidie? To sit inside and watch the races from the windows, where your toes will be warm and toasty, or stand at the finish line, where you'll have mud sprayed all over you?"

"The finish line." I followed him past the lines of people waiting to bet on the horses and went outside. The bleachers were less than half full; people sat under umbrellas or held folded newspapers over their heads.

We threaded our way to the railing, which was shiny and wet. It was raining harder now, and the track was thick with mud. Without thinking, I said, "Gallorette, the filly, hated a muddy track."

Rafael looked at me with surprise and nodded. "You're right. The winners today will be mudders, crazy horses who love a sloppy track."

I nodded. I knew that, too.

I pulled my hands into my jacket sleeves, shivering.

Rafael leaned closer. "Where is your scarf?"

I swallowed.

"You lost it?"

"It's in the bedroom." I saw the disappointment on his bony face. "I'll remember tomorrow."

I'd have to wear it. It was a good thing I wasn't going back to school. But how terrible to think I'd never be there again.

The horses were loaded into the gate for the first race. The bell clanged and the gate banged back. The horses thundered toward us, splashing up mud, the ground vibrating, the noise filling my ears, sounding even in my chest. I reached out and grabbed Rafael's arm as we both shouted in excitement.

In a blur, I saw the jockeys push back one set of goggles after another so they could see as the mud spattered their faces. Each rider must have been wearing five or six pairs.

And their silks! Each one wore an outfit whose color belonged to his stable. On a sunny day, they'd look like brightly colored birds, but today they were dark with mud as they rounded the turn.

A gray was far behind the rest. "Not a mudder," Rafael said. We watched her slosh along, and he shook his head. "That's Boston Star, a horse Pai trained. She likes solid ground under her feet. We should have scratched her, canceled her from the race, and waited to race her on a sunny day."

The race was close, two horses neck and neck at the finish line. We waited to see the name of the winner flash up on the screen, and then, as the horses left the field, I said, "You're going to ride your first race soon."

He didn't answer, and I turned to see something in his face. What was it?

But now there was shouting as the names went up on the scoreboard: Wait Awhile was first, Floribunda had placed second, and Blue Heron had shown in third. Rafael was talking about the money they'd made: some for the jockey, some for the trainer, some for the owner. . . .

But I didn't pay attention. All I was interested in was Wait Awhile coming around the side, and the look of pride on the jockey's face. "See that rider, Rafi?" I cut in.

"Go back to school, Lidie," he said.

I held up my hand. "Stop."

He said something else, but it was hard to hear with people shouting around us. *We can't always have what we want.* Was that what it was?

But there was too much noise; voices rang with excitement as the horses were funneled into the starting gate for the next race.

"A horse that Pai trained is running," Rafael said. "A chestnut named Storm Cloud. He's small, only a little more than fifteen hands, but feisty. Maybe we've got a chance."

I had a quick memory of Tio Paulo sitting on the porch in Jales. He'd held out his callused hand, running his finger across the widest part. *Four inches to a hand*, he'd said. *That's how they measure horses*.

We waited for the next race, our elbows on the wet railing. The bell rang and the starting gate shot open. The horses angled so close together it was hard to tell one from another, even though Rafael was pointing, trying to show me Storm Cloud.

Despite the mud, the race was fast; the horses galloped toward us in seconds, but as they rounded the turn, something happened. With an explosion of sound they came together, falling, a mass of brown and gray and muddy silks.

A screeching, keening sound came from one of the horses. Mud was everywhere, so much that I stood on tiptoes trying to see, my stomach lurching.

A jockey huddled near the rail, his cap gone, his mount continuing without him.

A chestnut horse was down on the track. Was it ours? Another horse bolted over him, and Rafael scaled the railing, darting around the horses, and threw himself toward the chestnut.

The crowd was shrieking, or maybe it was the sirens of the horse ambulance careening down the track. Horses were still milling around, and jockeys. I caught a glimpse of Rafael, deep in the mud, running his hands along the chestnut's foreleg.

"Crazy kid," someone said next to me. "He might have been killed."

And someone else: "Brave kid."

My brother. Brave.

I watched as he looked up to talk to the ambulance

driver, his hand still on the horse. In that moment, I realized he looked like Mamãe, and something else: how proud she'd be of him.

As he turned, I saw the worry in his eyes. I heard his voice in my head. *We can't always have what we want.* What had he meant?

12

THE FARM

After the track was cleared, we drove back to the farm and went into the barn.

"A miracle," Rafael told Pai. He looked like a raccoon; his face was filthy except for two lines on his cheeks that might have been tears. "I thought Storm Cloud had snapped his leg, but he'll be fine. Even Emilio, the jockey, was only bruised." He ran his hand over his muddy hair. "You'll see when José and the others bring him back in the van later."

I sat there on a stool, filthy myself but warm now, a mug of hot chocolate cupped in my hands. Around me were the smells of hay and leather from the tack room; nearby was a pyramid of green apples in a tub.

All the while, I kept glancing at Pai out of the corner of my eye. He looked stern, running his fingers through his graying hair, then bending to slap flecks of hay from his jeans. I kept asking myself what he'd say to me about leaving school. But maybe he wouldn't say anything, maybe he wouldn't even think about it with all the commotion over Storm Cloud. But that probably wouldn't be true, couldn't be true.

At last he stood in front of me. "What happened at school?"

I didn't answer.

He pulled at his upper lip, just the way Tio Paulo always pulled at his mustache. He went into the tack room, and I heard him banging things around.

"School is not important to you?" he asked as he came out. "How could you just walk out of there? Do you want to end up in some poor hovel because you can't read or write?" His eyes went to the ceiling.

I narrowed my eyes. "I can read very well, and write, too."

"But not in English. You're exactly as my brother Paulo said." He sighed. "A difficult girl."

Tio Paulo said that? What nerve! "You think Tio's not difficult? You should try living with him awhile."

Something flashed in his eyes. Was it laughter?

Suddenly I could see Mamãe's face, Mamãe laughing. My throat burned; I wished I could fold myself into her arms. I could almost feel her smoothing down my unruly hair. And the Horseman. Hadn't he laughed all the time, suddenly hugging Mamãe, hugging me?

No, I must have dreamed that.

Ah, Mamãe. Wouldn't she have said, *Don't worry. It's not so much of a thing, Lidie?*

But it *was* so much of a thing. All of it. What had happened, and what the others in the classroom had thought. And suppose the Horseman found out? Or Rafael? How terrible the shame would be!

At the far end of the barn, the door opened, and there was the teacher. I stared at her, willing her not to tell everyone. And at the same time, I knew that no matter what, I'd never go back to the school, never step into her classroom again.

She crouched in the hay in front of me and reached for my hands. She said words to me; sorry words, I thought.

I made my lips prisoners between my teeth and stared down at her hands, which were large and freckled.

She leaned over to ask the Horseman something, and he whispered the answer.

I heard her say *Lidie*, but the rest of it was impossible, and Pai repeated what she was trying to say.

"Come back!" How strange the Portuguese words sounded on her tongue. *"Come back, Lidie."* She rubbed my hands between hers.

I shook my head, and knew enough to say no in English.

"What is the matter with that girl?" The Horseman looked as if he'd explode.

"You're tired, Lidie." Rafael stood in front of the teacher and me now. "But I'll teach you English. Nothing to it." He waved his hand. "I will tell Mrs. Teacher the same thing." He turned and spoke to her, and she smiled, talking again.

Rafael told me what she was saying. "Sometimes hard things happen. We have to fix them the best we can."

"The best we can" is no good, I thought. But Rafael nodded. "And then you'll go back to school." He looked pleased.

I put on my *never* face.

"Maybe," Rafael said.

All this time the teacher was patting my hands. She said a long string of things to the Horseman, and he turned to me. "She says the children want you. She wants you. And nobody minds that you threw the math paper on the floor."

I gave the teacher a quick glance.

The Horseman's eyebrows went up. "Is this what it's all about? Math?"

The teacher turned so only I could see her face, so only I could see that quick wink, and to know what she was telling me without words. She hadn't told the Horseman; maybe she hadn't told anyone. She and Liz, the bee girl, knew, but maybe the drumming boy, Ian, and everyone else thought I'd left because of the math problems.

She stood up and shook hands with the Horseman, and then she was gone.

The Horseman slapped his hands on his knees. "See what a good teacher you have, and the children want you to come back." He smiled. "We have horses to take care of right now, but I myself will teach you math." He raised his eyebrows at Rafael. "Seven times nine, four times eight . . ."

I shrugged out of my jacket. "I know seven times nine, and seven times one hundred nine and—" I stopped. It wasn't even worth talking about.

But I didn't have to talk. I didn't have to say anything

more because there was the sound of a motor; the horse van was pulling up outside. "It's Storm Cloud," Rafael said.

We went outside as José turned the van toward the barn. I watched as Rafael and Pai helped unload the horse and lead him into the barn. "*Ai*," José said to Pai. "If you had seen Rafael, down in the mud, making sure Storm Cloud was all right, checking his legs . . ."

Rafael grinned, then put his hand on my shoulder.

"Come on, Lidie," he said. "I will teach you English, and at the same time you can help me." He opened the door to Storm Cloud's stall. "Move slowly," he said, holding up his hands. "He will frighten easily now. Be calm."

"I am calm." I slipped in behind him. "I'm always calm."

"Yes." He smiled. "You and Pai both."

He held up a comb and ran it over the chestnut's body in circles. "This is a currycomb." It will bring the mud up to the surface."

He handed me the currycomb and I began. The horse looked back at me with his large eyes, his long lashes. *Bom*, nice. The hay rustled as he moved a little. He leaned into the comb, his skin twitching slightly. I sang the lullaby that Mamãe used to sing about an angel coming, "*Nana, nenê, que o anjo vem pegar . . .*"

When I finished with the currycomb, Rafael gave me a brush. It was soothing to listen to the drip of water going automatically into Storm Cloud's bowl, to hear the soft swish of the brush as I ran it across his flanks and the sound of his contented breathing. It almost made me feel contented, too.

But then Rafael leaned over the half door, his face

serious. "So, Lidie, you must go to school. At least until you're sixteen." He came inside, lifting the horse's leg carefully, making sure there were no stones in his hoof. "It's the law," he said.

"I will go back to Jales first."

"If you go back to Jales . . . ," he began.

I raised my chin.

"You'll miss all the spring races. You'll miss seeing me ride."

I said it again, even though I wasn't sure. "I'll go back to Jales before then."

He shook his head and moved away. For the rest of the afternoon, we worked in the barn. I groomed another horse. No one spoke about school, or horses, or anything else. At supper, our heads were bent over our rice and beans until Rafael began to talk about the races, and Pai joined in.

Before I went to bed that night, I reached for the lemon on my dresser. It was streaked with brown, and my fingers left prints in the soft rind.

I brought it to my nose. It still had a sharp lemony smell, and I could picture Titia Luisa teaching me how to make a lemon pie, showing me how to roll out the dough, *lightly*, *lightly*, teaching me to add the sugar, *just a small scoop, Lidie*, then taste. *Ah, such a good baker, you're like your mother.*

But this lemon would never make a pie. This lemon was good for nothing.

I threw on my robe and went down to the kitchen on tiptoes, still holding it. Even at this hour of the night, it was easy to see. Outside, high overhead lights threw misty beams into the windows next to the table.

I stopped to peer out. The orange cat I had seen the first day was sitting on the fence. I would have knocked on the window to let her know someone else was around, but I didn't want to wake Pai or Rafael.

I stood there, the lemon in my hand for another moment, but then I buried it deep in the wastebasket so no one would ever see it again.

13

HARRISBURG, PENNSYLVANIA

The filly was alone.

She wanted the sun on her head, on her back, and a field where she might roll over in the sweet-smelling grass.

She pulled down the bag of oats that hung in front of her. When the creatures came near, she pawed the ground or kicked out at them until they jumped away.

She could see outside, but she was closed in. She was trapped, with no way to go back where she belonged.

If only she could run.

She longed to run.

Longed for something, but didn't even know what it was.

14

OUTSIDE HARRISBURG, PENNSYLVANIA

Saturday! I didn't have to think of what I'd do about school, not today, or even tomorrow. The wind rattled against my windows, but outside the sky was bright. It looked as if it would be a sunny day.

I rubbed my feet together under the quilt, which was stitched with pink bunnies. Rabbits again! But as I looked carefully, I saw it was probably Titia Luisa's needlework. I pretended she was the one who was warming my toes.

"Lidie, come downstairs. Hurry," the Horseman called from the bottom of the stairs. It was the first time he'd spoken since we were at the barn yesterday. All day he'd been quiet, his face closed.

I told myself I didn't care.

He came up, taking the steps two at a time, and tapped

on my bedroom door as he went past. "Get dressed," he called. "We're going to Pennsylvania, the three of us, to bring home two horses."

I could hear the excitement in his voice as he went down the hall and drummed on Rafael's door. "Rafael, wake up. Let's go."

I untangled myself from the quilt, threw on my jeans and a sweater, and went downstairs. In the living room, I stopped to glance in the mirror. I snapped on my hair clip, remembering the one I'd lost in the field that last day with Cavalo.

What were they were doing in Jales this minute? They'd e-mailed me last night, Tita Luisa telling me, "I miss you so," Tio saying, "You've probably forgotten us."

Oh, Tio.

I looked around, thinking how strange the living room looked. Its color was so sunny, and a lovely painting hung over the fireplace. It reminded me of the tree over the porch at home. But for the rest, it was nothing but a waiting room.

I went down the hall to the kitchen. "No time for a real breakfast, sorry," the Horseman said.

Instead we smeared *queijo*, wonderful soft cheese, on bread, and sipped hot cocoa before we rushed for our jackets.

I followed the Horseman and Rafael out the door, the wind on my face. Yesterday's rain had washed the last of the snow away.

But where were all the birds? There were only a few sparrows and a squawking starling lined up on the telephone wires as the truck lumbered out of the driveway and onto the expressway.

Almost no one was on the road this early. It was as if we were the only ones in the world, just the three of us inside the truck. I closed my eyes and swayed with its rhythm.

It was early for lunch, but we were hungry. When we were nearly there, the Horseman pulled over to the side of the road. Rafael opened a bag—pork sandwiches and a thermos of hot tea with milk.

I took my first bite as Pai began to talk. "We have to begin with your math."

"I don't need math," I said, my mouth full. "Thank you. I really know—"

"Can you divide?" he asked. It was as if I hadn't spoken.

I didn't answer. All I could think of was that terrible morning in school.

"So," he said, "if you were to divide seventy-two by twelve—"

"Six. Mrs. Figueiredo gave me the class medal for math last year."

He began with other numbers then, easy enough for a baby. What was the matter with everyone? I didn't want to listen.

I opened the window of the truck to a blast of wind, shutting out the sound of his voice. Papers and the sandwich wrappers flew over the seats. Rafael scrambled for them, then reached over me to close the window again.

What had made me do that? Was I was turning into a girl who looked just like the one in my passport? I stared out the window, pretending I was back in Jales.

Pai started the truck again as Rafael leaned forward to

turn on the radio. The music was Brazilian, and Rafael hummed along with it. After a while, I could feel my muscles begin to unclench. I was almost ready to say I was sorry when we bumped to a stop.

"This is the Bullington Farm," the Horseman said, as if the ride had been pleasant and no one had thought about dividing twelves and sixes.

The afternoon sun cast its light across a long red barn in a back field. Spread out in front of us were white fences and fields that that looked like pale green Titia Luisa quilts.

We slid out of the truck, and the wind blew my hair across my face and into my eyes. Two men came from the house to greet us, cups of coffee steaming in their hands, and a woman with streaked hair pulled open the barn doors, smiling.

She led us to a horse's stall. "We brought her in from South Carolina a couple of weeks ago. She's saddle broken and ready to go."

I stood there looking over the half door, caught by the filly's beauty. She was the color of the sky in Jales just before it stormed, a wonderful wild mix of black and white and gray. This horse had been born in the warmth of the South last year and brought here to this cold world, just as I had.

The horse turned to look at us—no, she looked at me. Her skin rippled, and then she moved uneasily as I stretched out my hand.

Her great dark eyes should have been shining, but they seemed dull to me; no, not dull. She was sad.

I drew in my breath. Wasn't that the look I'd seen in

68

Rafael's eyes, even though he was always smiling, always laughing?

I raised my hand to my face. Maybe I had that same look in my own eyes.

I reached out again and managed to touch her this time. But touching her gleaming side wasn't nearly enough. I wanted to put both my arms around her; I wanted to lean my head on her heavy mane. I couldn't believe we were taking her home, that I'd see her every day. . . .

And ride her.

Of course, I'd ride her.

I had a picture of the two of us in Jales: going through the high grass of the fields, over the rocks, and splashing through the *rio*.

"Shall we go to the other barn?" the woman was saying. "Don't you want to show your daughter . . ."

I followed them, looking back over my shoulder as the filly kicked at the stall wall.

"What's her name?" I asked the woman as I caught up with them.

"Wild Girl," she said.

I had a sudden pain in my chest, remembering Mamãe. She'd been watching me dance to a samba on television in her bedroom. I must have been five or six, making it all up as I went along.

My wild girl, she'd said.

And this horse—Wild Girl, too.

The Horseman stopped me just before we reached the doors of the red barn. "Lidie," he said, "school will work out. I don't want this moment spoiled—" He broke off. "This is for you. Rafael and I planned it. We've bought the perfect horse."

The woman swung back the heavy doors. Inside were several stalls, but all were empty except the one nearest to us.

Looking over the half door was a bay, her color almost the same as the mud on the track yesterday. Her ears were pricked forward: she was happy to see us.

I went closer and saw that she was swaybacked, her mane and forelocks sparse. Not a Thoroughbred, not a race horse, and ancient. Tio Paulo would have called her a backyard horse.

"She's yours, Lidie," the Horseman said.

I opened my mouth and closed it again. For a moment, laughter bubbled up inside my throat. This poor old horse for me.

The Horseman was waiting to hear what I'd say. I clenched my hands as I tried to think of something. I knew this was meant to be a wonderful gift.

"You can learn to ride on her," Rafael said. "She's safe, so safe. . . ."

"It'll be like sitting on a rocking chair," the woman said. "Perfect. She's sixteen years old. She's trained many riders."

They smiled as I went toward the stall. I opened the door and went inside, reaching up, feeling that soft muzzle, the bristly hairs on her chin, the veins that meandered along her flank like lines on a map.

"I knew she'd be thrilled," Rafael said. "This horse can live in the barn, and Lidie can take her out to the exercise track."

I rested my face against the horse's neck, that horse with

her dark teeth, her tired bones. Another ten pounds and I'd be too big for her.

Ai, *poor thing,* I could almost hear Titia Luisa saying.

"Her name is Love You," the woman said.

I ran my hand over the horse's ears and finally found something to say. "I love you, too, horse."

Everyone laughed then as we led her outside to the van. But under my laughing, I wished Pai had said it to me.

15

There wasn't much room in the van: hay to nibble on, water to
drink, and a wall separating the filly from another horse. She could
hardly see that horse, just her withers, a bit of her mane.

It reminded the filly of something.

Was it a field with sweet-smelling grass?

Hadn't there been other horses to run with?

And warm. Hadn't it been warm?

She looked back and caught a glimpse of the other horse's tail.
It was long, thick.

That reminded her of something, too.

Was it running? Was it stretching her nose to reach the end of
the field?

Or was it a mare?

She remembered something like that.

Still, it was hard to think about anything but this cold world.

16

THE BARN

On Sunday morning, the Horseman and Rafael sat at the kitchen table leaning over a piece of paper.

Rafael looked up. "Pai's giving me strategies for Doce's race. I'll be riding him."

I put myself in his place. How lucky to be riding that horse. To be racing. I leaned against the door, listening.

"Doce's a front runner." Pai tapped his pencil on the paper. "He's determined to be first, but sometimes he uses up his energy too quickly."

Rafael's head was tilted; he was nodding.

"You'll have to hold him back. Stay behind the lead horse, maybe in third or fourth place until the stretch." Pai looked at me. "That long, straight run before the finish." His hands curled into fists. "Then let him out, let him go."

"Tio Paulo told me about horses like that," I said. "In a short race you can give them their heads; in a longer race . . ."

They turned to look at me. "Right, Lidie." There was something in Pai's eyes, something I liked to see. He was smiling. "*Ai*, Paulo. He was a great rider when he was young. Better than all of us."

I thought about home. Tio Paulo might be outside, bending over the dark earth, inspecting his pole beans; Titia Luisa would be in the kitchen, her cheeks pink from the oven . . .

And what would I be doing?

Riding.

Racing Cavalo through the back roads, bringing up dust until I was coughing with it.

I looked at the heads bent over the papers and took a breath. "Can he win?" I asked.

They smiled at me, and Pai spread his hands wide. "Anything can happen in a race," he said. "Anything. The day, the horse, the jockey, the post position. It all has to come together."

And Rafael: "We'll draw for that post position before the race. Number one, next to the gate, would be a disaster for Doce. Everyone boxing us in, trying to get the lead against the rail. And just as bad would be way on the outside. We'd have to come all the way around the other horses. . . ."

"Seventh or eighth position," I said, not even realizing for a moment I'd heard that from Tio. "Let the others get ahead, and come straight down . . ." My voice trailed off.

Pai pushed back his chair. "Oh, Lidie. Yes."

And Rafael: "That's my girl."

I thought of something else but was too shy to say it. We didn't want rain; we didn't want mud. We wanted a nice hard, dry, fast track. I grinned at them. "Is it all right if I walk to the barn?"

"Fine," the Horseman said, back to studying his notes.

I went upstairs for my jacket and wrapped the bunny scarf around my neck so Rafael would be sure to see it. In the hall, I stopped to look at the painting of the chestnut horse and jockey. The painter had shown the horse's powerful legs stretched out, dust swirling up under its hooves. The jockey's arm was raised in victory.

As I went back down the stairs, I could hear the Horseman saying, "And to find a way to perk up Wild Girl."

I thought about the filly, her beautiful color, her long legs. There was time. She wouldn't race until she was two years old. Right now, I thought she might be lonesome. I knew how that was.

Downstairs, I stopped to take a roll of peppermints I'd seen in the kitchen drawer and let myself out of the quiet house. Outside, it wasn't as quiet: José was exercising Storm Cloud, whose hoofs pounded down the exercise track. A flock of crows cawed in the trees beyond the fence. I caught a glimpse of the orange cat, on her way somewhere, her tail high. She looked at me, then kept going.

I went into the barn, first to see the old horse, Love You. She was contented in her stall, chewing on a clump of hay, her large jaws working as she turned to see me. I let myself inside and began to brush her, listening to the *drip-drip-drip* of the water in her pail.

She was a lovely old horse, and she could live here for many years, in a stable where there was plenty to eat and cool water to drink and other horses to see. Her stall was warm and the golden hay under her feet was fresh.

Smiling a little, I pictured her leaning over her half door when all was quiet, having conversations with the other horses. *Nice exercise this morning,* she might say, or *What did you think of breakfast?*

I thought again about what it would be like to go back to Jales, to fly across the field calling for Cavalo. I tried to brush the thought away as I brushed the dust from Love You's flanks and lifted her hooves to be sure there were no pebbles caught in her shoes.

I finished with the soft brush and gave her one of the peppermints from my pocket. Cavalo's owner, the farmer, had taught me that horses loved them. *Peppermints remind the horses of the fields with the smell of mint, the taste of the leaves,* he'd said once.

She chewed it with her thick yellow teeth, then nosed my hand for another one.

"Just one more." I gave it to her, leaving her stall with that minty smell behind me.

At last I went down to the end, to Wild Girl's stall. I walked fast; I was anxious to see her. Her eyes were half closed, when I wished she'd been leaning over her door, her ears pricked with curiosity.

"A Sunday nap," I said to her softly. "Did they exercise you this morning?"

She turned to look at me. I opened her door and went

inside slowly, a clean currycomb in one hand and a pepper-mint in the other.

I knew she could smell the mint; I saw the curious look as she brought her head around.

"Gotcha," I said, and opened my hand, the candy on my palm.

She thought about it; then I felt her muzzle on my hand as she took it.

I started with the currycomb, moving in circles against her wonderful gray body, the veins underneath like the ripples of the *rio* at home.

She began to relax, to move into the comb as I went. I sang "*Nana, nenê*"—"Sleep, baby"—and the water dripped into her bucket as a pale sun came in the window behind us.

And suddenly I was talking to her, really talking, not just horse talk or baby talk. "Here's everything," I told her. "I tried not to think of how much I wanted a family, not just to hang out at Titia Luisa and Tio Paulo's. I wanted the Pai who had held me up to the lemon tree. I wanted to belong." I was surprised at myself. I'd never really thought it all out before. "But I don't feel as if this is really a family."

I didn't want to think about Pai and the lemon tree now. I leaned against her. "Oh, Wild Girl," I said, "even if I don't belong here in America, you do."

I was silent then, and Wild Girl turned her head, looking at me.

I reached into my pocket and pulled out another peppermint.

"I love the way your eyes look," I said. "And I'd try to ride you, but can you imagine what Pai would say?"

I told myself I didn't care.

I went to work on Wild Girl's mane, and then I couldn't help myself. I stood on a box and held on to that mane as I tossed myself up on her broad back.

I put my head down on her neck and crooned to her, crooned to myself.

It was something, not everything, but the happiest moment I'd had since I'd come here to New York.

17

THE BARN

The filly felt the taste of the strange food in her mouth long after she'd swallowed. It was a good taste, the taste of a field on a summer day.

One of the creatures had come into her space. The noises it made were soft. It had brushed her side until her skin rippled with its good feeling.

And when the creature had climbed up on her, the filly had barely felt its weight, just its warmth.

It was something. . . .

It wasn't like being in the field with other horses, but still . . .

Something.

18

THE EXERCISE TRACK

I stopped to e-mail Tio Paulo. I told him that America was wonderful and school was exciting. I didn't feel one bit guilty, even though *exciting* wasn't exactly the right word. Besides, Tio was the one who was always said how great it would be in America.

Then I went up to sit on the bedroom floor, leaning against the baby-pink wall.

"Lidie?" Rafael called, rapping on the door.

I couldn't open it. How could I let him see that Snow White and those seven dwarfs were mostly covered with pictures of horses? It looked as if Big Brown were dangling from Snow White's dainty fingers.

"I'll be right down."

"Never mind *right down*," he said. "How about timing me on Doce?"

"Why not?" I opened the door just far enough to squeeze through and followed Rafael downstairs and outside along the path.

He took my arm and began to talk about school.

I didn't want to hear any of it.

"When I first came," he said, "I knew about three words of English, and none of them were any use. Everyone laughed. I couldn't even find the bathroom."

I didn't look at him. But I told myself there was no way that he knew what had happened to me.

"Then I began to pick up words. I didn't even know where they came from." He glanced at me. "And some of the kids thought it was cool that I could speak another language."

I didn't answer, but he knew I was thinking about it.

At the barn, he glanced at his watch. "Want a riding lesson on Love You before you time me?"

I shook my head. The first time he saw me ride, it wouldn't be on Love You. It would be on a fast horse, a Thoroughbred. It would be Wild Girl.

I heard him say something about not being afraid as he strapped on his helmet and saddled Doce.

He handed me the stopwatch as I followed them along to the exercise track. The orange cat sat next to the gate, and I saw she had six toes on each of her front paws. I reached out slowly and ran my hand over her rough back.

Rafael brought Doce around the track once; they went slowly, almost meandering. They came toward me then. He waved, and they began!

As they galloped by, the sudden wind blew against my face, and the sound of Doce's hooves vibrated in my chest.

I could almost feel myself on the horse, sensing the movement with my arms and legs, Doce's mane flying, the sound of his breathing, the feel of my own breathing. He was faster than Cavalo, much faster.

Rafael had more grace than I would have imagined. He was almost one with the horse. It was thrilling to watch as he guided the horse close to the rail, and I forgot the stopwatch, forgot that I was supposed to be timing him.

I couldn't take my eyes off him. The orange cat came up to me, and I picked her up and began to work out a burr behind her ears with my fingers.

The way Rafael rode reminded me of the painting in the hall: the horse's legs extended, the dust in swirls under his feet. For the first time, I realized that the horse in the painting was actually Doce, and Rafael was the jockey. Had Rafael painted it? Had Rafael painted the other pictures, too? The one in the living room and the one in the barn of Native Dancer?

Rafael turned Doce, trotting back toward me, and saw my face. "You were wonderful, really fast," I said. I looked down at the stopwatch. "Sorry, I forgot . . ."

He raised one shoulder helplessly, and of course, he laughed.

"You were fast. So fast." I thought of Tio Paulo. "You were born to ride."

His face changed, and I saw the look in his eyes. Was it a sad look? Maybe he was worried about his race coming up? His first race. Maybe he was worried about losing, and what Pai might say.

But I forgot about that as I watched him grooming Doce back in the barn, still talking about school and how wonderful it would be for me.

At home, we went back into the kitchen. Pai was scrambling eggs and stirring a pot with beans and molasses, and Rafael poured himself a cup of coffee.

And I tried not to think about school.

19

WOODHILL SCHOOL

On Monday morning, I went to school after all. I really didn't have a choice.

"I'll take you," Rafael said, standing in the kitchen, making lunch for me again.

But I shook my head. "Thanks, I'm fine. I'll walk."

"Good. I want to help with the exercising." He made pointers of his fingers, reminding me of the way: straight to the end of our road, two blocks left, another one right.

At the table, the Horseman glanced up from his newspaper. "I could take you."

"I'm all right," I said.

"The math. We forgot." His hand went to his upper lip. "Paulo said that you're smart, that your teacher said you can do anything—" He broke off. "I don't understand what happened the other day."

I tried to think of what to say that would bring us away from that morning.

"Don't worry," I said. "The math will be fine." I narrowed my eyes. "You'll see." I was going to do something about math today, no matter what.

"And English, too," he said. "Don't forget about the English."

One thing after another.

I didn't answer him. *Days of the week; the tree is nice; I'm hippy to be here; watch out, the mosquito bites.*

I nodded at them both. "After school, I'll take care of Love You. Don't worry about that, either," I said, and let myself out the door.

I went along the driveway, looking back to see José on one of the chestnuts, then took the long road to the end where it turned. I practiced what I was going to say to Mrs. Bogart, mumbling to myself.

I passed the fruit store, but it wasn't open yet. There was a sign on the door, BACK ON MONDAY.

The words came into my head. A weekend sign. And I knew what it meant.

"Back on Monday," I said aloud. "And Tuesday, Wednesday, Thursday."

And another sign. FRESH APPLES.

Ah.

Soon the school was ahead, and I saw the drumming boy, Ian, up ahead, talking to someone and waving his arms around, but I didn't see anyone else from our class. Never mind. I knew my way to the classroom, too.

I went down the hall and straight to the teacher's desk, waiting while she wrote something on a pad in front of her.

At last she looked up. "Lidie. I'm glad to see you."

I said it slowly: "I know math."

"Yes, good."

I said it again, realizing I'd forgotten a word. "I know *hard* math."

She tilted her head, said something, but I caught none of it.

"I want—" I began.

"Hard math," she said.

She went to my desk and sat down next to me, a thick book in her hand. She gave it to me to look through, waiting patiently.

It began with the easiest adding problems, baby subtraction, and I thumbed through the pages. Halfway through, I went back a few pages.

I picked up a pen and worked out the problems on that page, X equals this, Y equals that. I couldn't do the ones that had long English questions, but no matter. I skipped over them.

I did a few on the next page, then moved forward two or three pages, and kept going until I didn't know any more.

I looked up to see Liz standing there with a few others, watching me. Mrs. Bogart smiled at them. "Wow," she said.

I knew from the sound of this word *wow* that I had done well, really well.

"Wow," I said, too, and they all laughed, but the laughing was kind. Mrs. Bogart went to her closet and brought me another math book to put in my desk. She patted it. "For you."

Girls spoke to me now, interrupting each other, still talking as if I were deaf, but I was smiling, smiling, and so were they.

"Library," Mrs. Bogart said.

I looked at Liz. I wondered if I knew that word.

"Books," Liz said.

Ah, *biblioteca*.

We lined up at the side of the room, on our way to the library.

I passed my hooded jacket on its hook, with its slight bulge in one sleeve, the baby scarf that no one could see. Maybe my jacket belonged there after all; maybe I did, too.

Upstairs, we went through double doors. The librarian was a man with wavy gray hair; he looked as if he liked to eat. "Hello, Lidie," he said, and placed a thick book in my hands, a book with pictures.

I drew in my breath. I had seen this book many times before, but now the words were in English.

I paged through. It began with a picture of a herd of horses running together, all legs, a cloud of dust behind them.

I thought of Tio Paulo's words: *They came from herds, living with horses all around them. And even though it was thousands of years ago, they haven't forgotten. They need friends.*

A few pages later, I saw Gallorette, the famous tomboy filly. On another page, I saw Ruffian, queen of the fillies.

I sat there the whole period with Liz, saying their names.

Then I saw the photo of Native Dancer. "I have . . . ," I told Liz.

"The horse?" she asked.

"No, not the horse." I tried not to laugh. "The . . ."

I reached for the word, and suddenly it was there. "The picture."

And then we both laughed. "Look," she said, reading, then pointing to the blur in the corner. "Isn't that a cat?"

"Yes, the cat was . . ."

I stopped.

The cat was his friend. The whole sentence came to me in English.

But then the time was up. I held the book to my chest when the librarian reached for it.

It was so hard to let it go. It was almost as if I'd sat in the library at home in Jales. But after I handed it to him, I watched to see where he put it. I wanted to be able to find it again.

We walked back to the classroom, and all the while I was thinking.

Suddenly I knew what Wild Girl needed.

A cat. A friend.

And I knew just where to find one.

I could imagine Wild Girl changing, becoming feisty, happy. Just as exciting, I thought of what Pai would say when he saw what had happened.

I hugged the thought of it to myself for the rest of the school day. A cat, of course. It was so easy, so perfect, I couldn't stop smiling.

20

THE STALL

The sun beamed through the window over the filly's head.

She ate the warm mash from her pail, raising one hoof and then the other. Then she poked her head over the half door of her stall . . .

And waited.

Would the creature come again? The one with the thick mane of hair, the one who weighed almost nothing on her back?

The filly's ears pricked forward, listening for the sound of those quick footsteps.

Waited.

21

THE FARM

I sat on the floor in my room, my head back against the wall, trying to keep my eyes open. I had to be sure Pai and Rafael were asleep. Bringing the cat to Wild Girl had to be a surprise.

I thought I'd never hear them come upstairs. We'd all sat in the kitchen, talking until long after bedtime about Rafael's first race and how Doce would run. I'd finally said goodnight, trying to give them the idea it was time to sleep.

When everything was quiet at last, I slipped out of the bedroom and tiptoed down the hall. I stopped at the small lighted lamp on the table to look at the painting of the horse and jockey. I rubbed my bare foot against my leg, pretending I was the jockey racing my horse to the finish line. I thought again of Rafael's first race tomorrow, how hard he was working. He was out on the exercise track every chance he had.

Downstairs, I rummaged through the cabinets, trying to decide what a cat might like for a midnight snack. Titia Luisa would have thought it was a terrible kitchen. There wasn't enough food to keep a family of mice alive.

I remembered there was a little leftover fish from dinner in the refrigerator. It was dry and chewy; Rafael had cooked it to leather. I didn't think the cat would complain, though.

I scooped up the fish plate and a few mushy vegetables, grabbed my jacket off the hook, my striped boots from the floor underneath, and went out the back door.

The lights threw misty beams across the barn roof and over the exercise track. How beautiful it was at night! I looked back at the windows; inside, there was just the faintest light from that hall lamp, but the outside walls, the door, and the steps were sharp and clear.

I took a breath. "Here, kitty," I called, trying to keep my voice down.

The cat was nowhere to be seen. But the other day I had watched her go over the fence and into the small grove of trees out back. I crossed the track and opened the back gate. Under the outline of branches it was dark. Really dark. The ground was as mushy as the cooked vegetables; there was a thick layer of damp leaves from last year.

I'm not afraid, I told myself. *I'm wild as a cat, wild as anything that could be creeping around.* I moved from one tree to the next, waving the plate with the fish in the air.

"Where are you?" I called. "Where have you gotten yourself?"

"I'm right here," a voice said in my own Portuguese.

I dropped the fish and jumped back, banging into a tree trunk. A woman stood there in the dark, a big woman. Her hair was caught up in a mess of a topknot on her head, her hands on her hips.

The light was too dim for me to see her face, but her voice was loud. "What are you doing?" she said. Was her voice angry? Surprised?

No more surprised than I was.

I turned and scrambled through the gate, realizing that my lovely boot had come off my foot and was somewhere in the leaves behind me. But never mind the boot or the fish with its mushy vegetables, never mind the cat for now.

Halfway across the track, I looked back, but I didn't see anyone. Maybe I'd dreamed it all. My hand went up to my chest, and I stood there, head down; I took deep breaths, trying to steady myself.

Half asleep, I told myself. That was *all* it was.

I hesitated. Should I go back again to look for the cat and my boot?

I sighed. I'd have to wait until tomorrow. I'd do it in the daytime. I wasn't as wild as I'd thought I was. I let myself back into the house and locked the door behind me, then took two peppermints from the kitchen drawer. I went upstairs with one in each cheek, sucking on them.

No wonder the horses liked them. The minty taste was calming.

"Is that you, Lidie?" Pai called from his bedroom, his voice sleepy.

I didn't answer. Quickly I opened my door, slipped inside,

and closed it behind me. I waited before I moved, counting in my head to a hundred.

He didn't call again, so I moved across the room. I took a quick look out the window. At first, I didn't see anything. But there, on the fence, was the orange cat. I couldn't believe it. Where had she come from?

I watched for another few minutes, but there was no one else outside. I dropped my jacket and the one boot on the floor, then climbed into bed.

22

THE RACE

I had no time to think about the cat or the dream woman in the forest. It was a busy day in school, with music and a play in the auditorium.

I left school the minute the dismissal bell rang and ran almost all the way to the track, feeling the warm sun on my head. Rafael would ride Doce in the ninth race!

I wore the same coral shirt I'd worn that day I'd flown from Brazil. "My favorite color," I'd told Rafael this morning. "It will bring you luck; I know it will."

"Not pink?" he said. "I thought it was pink. We talked Mrs. Januário into that color for the stable. I'll be wearing pink silks."

I suddenly realized he'd chosen it for me, and swallowed. "Pink," I said. "Yes, of course. Pink, too."

I ran past the stone pillars, waving my pass at the guard, and went straight to the paddock where the jockeys would mount. Stable hands were leading Doce into the area. Doce's mane was carefully braided, his face mask and socks in matching pink.

Pai and Rafael walked along behind them, heads together, going over the things they'd talked about at dinner last night.

Rafael! He looked so different. I hardly knew him. A jockey. Splendid in his silks. Walking along as if he'd done this forever. And Pai! For the first time I saw him wearing a jacket and tie.

I crossed my fingers: *Let Rafael win, please let him come in first.* I waved, and he raised one finger to his helmet.

I thought of myself then. How would it be if I were the one entering the paddock area? I'd be the one up on Doce, watching his head turning from side to side.

When Rafael mounted Doce, I knew how I would feel: mouth dry, heart beating fast; telling myself I was going to win, had to win, that I wanted that more than anything.

Someday it would be me, I was sure of it. I'd make it happen. I'd work so hard, learning everything there was to know about horses and riding. In my mind was a picture of Tio Paulo rocking on the porch, telling me about his own first race years ago, then glancing at me: *And you were born to ride.*

Would Rafael win his first race? And someday, would I?

Rafael went past, up on Doce, his helmet low over his forehead. Then I hurried with Pai to our place in the grandstand, moving around knots of people. The stands were half empty because the race was late in the afternoon; it was easy for our eyes to sweep across the track. And what I saw, next to our seats, what I could hardly believe I saw, was the woman with the topknot of hair from last night.

As we angled our way toward her, I heard the announcer's deep voice: *"The horses are on the track."*

I turned to Pai, but he was watching for that first glimpse of Rafael as they loaded the horses into the gate.

I looked toward the gate and saw our first bit of luck. Rafael's post position was number seven—not too close to the rail, where he'd be crushed in; not too far out, where he'd have to angle his way past the others.

Next to me was the woman, smiling a little. "A good position," she said.

Pai leaned toward her. "Mrs. Januário," he said. "I'm so glad you're back, so glad you could see Rafael up on Doce." He put his hand on my shoulder. "This is my daughter, this is Lidie."

Mrs. Januário. The owner of the stable.

"A night creature, like me," she said softly. Pai, glancing at the starting gate, didn't seem to hear her. "I put your boot on the back step."

I raised my shoulders helplessly and whispered a thank-you.

Pai glanced toward us. "Mrs. Januário came from São Paulo with her parents years ago."

I nodded. So that was why she sounded like us.

Now I turned to the gate, my hands icy for Rafael. I tried not to think about what it would be like if Doce ran out of steam, if they trailed along behind that field of horses, or were boxed in where they couldn't break out ahead of the others. I crossed my fingers: *"Come in first,"* I whispered. *"Win."*

I didn't have time for more than that quick worry. The bell rang, and the gates banged open. The horses were out, running, thundering toward us, a blur of bodies and legs and jockeys high up on their mounts. I kept my eye on that bit of pink: Rafael, helmet down, goggles down, one with Doce.

The lead horse was about a furlong ahead—maybe an eighth of a mile—and the others were bunched up behind him when three cut away and moved toward the lead horse.

I knew Rafael was holding Doce back. It was something Pai had said again this morning: *Don't make your move until the final turn.* And Rafael was responding as if Pai's thoughts and his were one.

Then it was time. Rafael asked Doce to go, and Doce responded instantly.

Everything was blurred for me as Doce reached the horses in front of him. It almost seemed as if he'd have to create his own space to move through them.

I found myself whispering, *"Anything can happen, anything—"*

We jumped to our feet as one of the horses clipped the heels of another. The rider was thrown from his saddle!

The horse went diagonally across the track, slowing down the others. It gave Rafael enough room to squeeze through, around the horse, and around the rider, who had darted out of the way of the horses.

Fast, then. It was all so fast. I grasped Pai's arm, my fingers digging into him, hardly realizing what I was doing, yelling, "Rafi, Rafi!" as he closed the gap, passing the third horse, and the second.

He was so close behind the first, so close . . .

And then he was neck and neck with that first horse. Rafael was crouched down on Doce's back, the reins tight as they crossed the finish line.

But who had won?

Next to me, Pai grasped the railing, and Mrs. Januário was yelling, "Doce, was it Doce?"

In the infield, the sign lighted up: PHOTO.

We waited; the crowd waited. Behind us, people were shouting.

Pai turned to me. "Inside, they're looking at photos of the finish line. They'll study them from every angle." He tilted his head, his mouth not quite steady. "Ah, wouldn't it be something if . . ."

He never finished. The answer was up on the board for us.

I began to cry. I was crying from the excitement, crying because I loved Rafael, crying because, by just a nose, he had won!

Mrs. Januário was shouting "Yes!" in her deep voice. Pai's face was blurred by my tears. He grabbed my hand and we ran to be there, to see Rafael, his arm raised high over his head in a victory salute.

23

THE STABLE

It wasn't until the next morning that I thought about the orange cat. The rest of the afternoon had been one I'd always remember: Rafael, his helmet slung over one arm, filthy from the dirt of the track, grabbing us both to him, smiling, laughing.

I couldn't stop crying. It was almost as if all the tears I'd saved up since the two of them had left Jales were seeping out of me.

Seeing Pai's face, I wondered that I'd thought he had no feeling. He threw his arms around me, around Rafael, and we went out to dinner afterward to celebrate. Mrs. Januário came with us for pizza with sausages and onions, and a green salad as crisp as Titia Luisa's. We toasted Rafael and Doce and talked together about the race, all of it, over and over.

They argued, laughing, over who would pay for dinner. Now that Doce had won, they'd all have a little money.

Mrs. Januário leaned toward me, her head next to mine. "Why were you . . . ," she began.

"I was looking for the cat."

Her eyebrows went up. "I was, too. Poor thing out there without a decent meal."

We smiled at each other.

"Horses and cats," she said. "We have a lot in common."

Today in school we had library again. I found my horse book on the shelf, and Liz and I paged through it together. I lingered over a photo of Seabiscuit with his friend, the trainer "Silent Tom" Smith, and thought about bringing the orange cat to Wild Girl.

The dismissal bell rang. I walked along the avenue toward home, waving to the man in the fruit store. His windows were lined with pots of daffodils, and shoots of green covered the tree branches across the street.

This afternoon I'd find the cat, even if I had to look for her until it was dark. I'd see the sudden spark in Wild Girl's eyes, the beginning of a friendship that would change everything for her.

What would Pai say? He'd reach out to me, and I'd tell him about the book, about Native Dancer and his stray black cat.

At home, I dropped my books in the doorway. I knew Pai and Rafael would be at the track. I went outside, calling, *"Here, kitty kitty; here, orange cat,"* stopping to see if she'd appear.

In front of the barn, José slept on a three-legged stool,

his mouth open. I gave Love You a carrot, and she grazed my shoulder with her muzzle. "I'll be back to see you later," I told her.

I gave one to Wild Girl as well. "This is the day that will change your life."

I went outside again, and there, at last, was the cat, walking along the exercise track on her fat orange paws, her tail held high. I called to her again.

She stopped and I went toward her, scooping her up, my face to her rough fur.

I walked inside the barn and saw Wild Girl's head over the top of her half door. I knew what it was like to feel alone. I knew that terrible ache.

The horse and cat would be together in that warm hay that smelled sweetly of the outdoors. I imagined Wild Girl on the track with the cat perched on the railing.

I listened to the cat purr as we reached the stall.

But only for a moment.

There was an explosion of sound as Wild Girl threw back her head and kicked out.

The other horses in their stalls sensed her fear. They whinnied, kicked. A pail went over with a clatter, and José came running back.

The cat flew out of my arms, leaving scratches on my wrist as she shot down the aisle and out the barn doors.

Before I could take a breath, Pai was standing in the doorway. *"What have you done?"*

My mouth was so dry, I couldn't begin to think of an answer.

Instead, I ran. I followed the cat down the driveway past Mrs. Januário's house and turned into the road.

24

THE BARN

The filly's heart was pounding.

The small creature with sharp teeth and claws that ripped had come into her space!

The filly screamed. She kicked out, kicked and missed the creature. She felt the fear begin in the others around her, heard their movement, their sounds.

If she could have run she would have, but she was trapped inside.

Then the creature was gone, and there was only the sound of her own whinnying and the noise of the others as they moved in their stalls.

She trembled, trying to quiet herself.

25

THE DINER

I saw the truck coming slowly along the avenue; then Rafael pulled up next to me. He leaned over and opened the door. In a voice that reminded me of Mamãe, he said, "It's really not so much of a thing, Lidie."

I shook my head.

"Come on," he said. "Get in."

I slid in, barely glancing at him.

He put his hand on my shoulder. "I don't know why that horse spooked, but horses have long memories, really long, stronger than their hearing, and much stronger than their vision." He spread his hands wide. "So who knows? But listen, the horses have calmed down. We gave all of them treats. . . ."

I sat there, head bent, not answering.

"I want to go home." My voice was so low I was surprised that he heard me.

"Sure."

I shook my head. "I mean—"

"You mean you'd like to stop at the diner first for an English muffin? A Danish? A hot chocolate?" His head was tilted, his smile crooked. "Maybe with a marshmallow or whipped cream on top?"

It was hard not to smile back at him, but I looked away. "That's not what I meant."

"I remember what you looked like the day Pai and I left Jales. You were sitting on the steps crying. . . ." He waved his hand in front of his face. "You were wearing pink overalls. You loved those overalls."

I hadn't thought about those overalls in years. I'd wait on the laundry room steps for them to come out of the wash. I closed my eyes: pale pink buttons that looked like flowers, a scroll of rosebuds around the bottoms of the legs.

I'd never worn those overalls again after that day. I'd watched the car drive away, and I'd gone down to the *rio*, splashing through the water all the way to the rocks. By the time Titia Luisa found me, I was covered with mud and had lost one of those flower buttons.

Ah, child, she'd said, *it's not that he doesn't love you. How could he take care of such a little girl like you?*

I never believed her.

"You loved pink," Rafael said now.

I looked up at him, and he nodded. Another pain in my chest. "The pink silks." I took a breath. "And that's why you

112

painted the bedroom pink." How disappointed he must have been when I hardly said two words about it. "I'm sorry, Rafael, I didn't remember."

"And Snow White and her dwarfs," he said. "You had a book you read over and over."

It was even harder to remember that. A fat little book? Snow White with her hand outstretched, a bluebird on her fingers? Was that it?

"I was waiting for that girl to get off the plane," he said. "Somehow I was expecting that little kid we'd left on the steps in Jales."

Was I going to cry again?

"I'm going to paint something else on your wall," he said. "It'll be a surprise. You'll be able to live with it for years."

"Never mind," I said, and wiped my eyes and my cheeks, trying to stop the tears. "I like Snow White, I do. Really."

"That's what Pai said."

Before I could say anything else, he began to drive. "Home is here with us," he said. "Nowhere else. It's where you belong. And right now we're going to the diner."

"All right."

"We'll get ourselves a snack because it's Pai's turn to cook tonight, and you know his dinners are much worse than mine."

I reached for a tissue, then realized I was starving.

"And it will give him a little time to calm down," Rafael said.

It was almost dinnertime, so the diner was filled with people, but we found a booth next to the window.

With the sweet tea and buttery English muffins we'd or-
dered, I began to feel better. *It's not so much of a thing,
Lidie*.

"I'll tell you something," I said, "if you tell me something
back."

"It depends," he said.

"Say yes."

"All right, yes."

"I can ride," I said, the words spilling out. "I can really
ride. Maybe not as well as you, but still . . ."

I took a sip of that warm tea to slow myself down. "I rode
all over Jales on the farmer's horse, Cavalo. Sometimes I saddled him; sometimes I rode bareback. We climbed the steep
rocks on the other side of the *rio* all the time—"

I broke off and began again. "Tio Paulo said I was born to
ride."

"Who can believe Tio Paulo?" Rafael said, but I knew he
was teasing me.

"It's true," I said. "I'm small enough, and in a few years
I'm going to be a jockey. I'm going to ride horses like Big
Brown and Rags to Riches. You'll see. In the meantime, I'll
ride Wild Girl if she ever perks up."

For a moment, I saw sadness in Rafael's face, but then he
raised his eyebrows. "You didn't need to learn on Love You?"
He sat back, shaking his head, smiling.

"That poor old horse," I said, and we laughed together.

I looked down at my cup, trying to think of how I'd ask
him what I wanted to know. Then I blurted it out. "Tell me
what's wrong, Rafael."

He shook his head. "What could be wrong? The tea's not too hot, the English muffin's not too cold. . . ."

I held up my hand. "Stop." But he wasn't looking at me. His head was bent, the cup up to his mouth.

"You haven't touched the English muffin anyway. Rafael, I know there's something."

He put down the cup. He was trying to smile. "I was born to ride, too."

"I know that. I could see it."

"I'm too big," he said. "Pai doesn't know it yet, or if he does, he doesn't want to think about it."

I shook my head. "What do you mean?"

"The good jockeys are all about a hundred pounds, maybe just a little more." He put the cup down. "I weigh more than that now, and even though I'm starving myself, my bones are getting heavier, I'm too tall. . . ."

He looked out the window. "I have this season. But by the fall, it'll be too late."

"No," I said, but I saw his wrists and his shoulders. He was right. You could see how wide he was, bigger than anyone in our family.

We sat there, not talking for a while.

"What are you going to do?" I asked.

"I'm going to ride now," he said. "Tomorrow, and the rest of this meet. I can do that. Pai is so proud, I feel . . ."

"Then?"

He raised his shoulders. "Who knows?" He was trying to smile.

I held my warm cup to my mouth.

"Sometimes," he said, "when you've been dreaming about something for a long time, and it doesn't turn out the way you expected . . ." He stopped.

I nodded. I knew what he meant. Of course I did. Wasn't that what was happening to me?

Rafael left money on the table, and we drove home together, not saying a word.

26

WOODHILL SCHOOL

The next morning, I hurried down the hall toward my classroom. Before school, I'd been up early, and outside. I'd stood at the track watching Rafael and the others exercise the horses. I caught a glimpse of Wild Girl at the far end, José working her easily, and Mrs. Januário riding Doce, her hair down, her head up to the morning breeze.

I suddenly realized I was late. I ran, knowing I couldn't make school by the bell, and was the last one in the door.

Today the classroom had been rearranged. The tables lined the sides of the room, and Mrs. Bogart was unrolling a purple rug in the center of the floor.

She saw me in the doorway and beckoned. I went into the room, and Liz grabbed my hand and showed me

117

where our seats were. "Chair," she said, patting the back of it.

I slid into the seat and looked around. Someone was watering plants on the windowsill: a geranium that was beginning to flower, and a green vine that twirled around a trellis made of straws.

Mrs. Bogart said something and clapped her hands. It must have been *Come*, because everyone went toward her and sat on the purple rug. I went with them, sinking down next to Liz.

Mrs. Bogart was smiling at me, I could see that. And in front of her was a pile of small books. She said something then that sounded almost like my own language. I repeated it in my head, trying to figure it out.

She said it again. "*Eu quero . . .*"

Yes. Her accent was strong, but still I understood her. "I want . . . ," she said.

She leaned forward, her hands out, looking at me.

Next to me, Liz was frowning.

"What?" Ian asked.

Mrs. Bogart winked at me. "*Eu quero*"—she looked up at the ceiling—"*cachorro quente.*"

Hot dog? Was that what she meant? I began to laugh. "*É mesmo!*" I said back without thinking. *Really.*

Everyone looked at me as Mrs. Bogart gave out the books, which I saw were Portuguese-English dictionaries. There weren't enough to go around, so we had to share.

Mrs. Bogart pointed at me. "*Tu queres . . .*"

What did I want? Ice cream, maybe. *"Sorvete."*

Around me, everyone was paging through the books, leaning over each other's shoulders. Everyone wanted to be the first to find what we'd said.

Then Ian had it. "Ice cream," he said.

I tried to fit my tongue around those sounds. *I want ice cream.*

Gradually everyone caught on. Liz wanted earrings, Ian wanted a drum, someone else wanted summer, all of them trying it in dreadful Portuguese that made me laugh, and they laughed, too.

I began to separate their faces in my mind: Ashley with the dark hair, Will with all the freckles, Kathy who sat on the other side of me.

In spite of everything, I was glad to be in that classroom with the straggly geranium on the windowsill and the puffy jackets hanging on the hooks at the side of the room. My jacket was exactly in the middle, and I thought it might be happy to be there, too, in this noisy classroom.

Mrs. Bogart made circular motions with her hands as she looked at her watch. We rushed to roll up the rug and put the little books in a pile on her desk. And then, on my way to my seat, I looked up at her. I felt tears come into my eyes and brushed them away. Crying again!

Mrs. Bogart nodded at me as if she knew I was thanking her. And then she passed out pieces of yellow paper with lines. *"Eu quero . . . ,"* she said.

I looked around to see everyone bent over the papers,

beginning to write. An essay. We'd done those a thousand times in Jales. Mrs. Bogart came down to my desk and touched the paper with her finger. "Write in Portuguese."

I sat there thinking about it. Whatever I'd write would be secret; no one would know what it said without a dictionary. It was almost a magic language, and I was the only one here who knew it.

I could say anything. I could even say the truth.

I picked up my pen. I wrote that I wanted everything to be the way I thought it was, all those years in Jales when I sat on the front porch thinking about America. Never mind Rafael telling me sometimes things weren't as we expected.

I wanted Rafael to be happy; I wanted to be happy.

I grinned to myself as I thought I wanted a decent meal and a house that was noisy.

I wanted Wild Girl to love the barn and the training track.

And Pai.

I dug into the paper with my pen. I wanted this Pai to disappear and the old Pai who laughed with Mamãe to come back. I wanted a Pai who remembered the lemon.

How could he have forgotten?

Ian came around to collect the papers, and I looked at my terrible essay: the pen had followed all the angry thoughts in my head.

Ian glanced over my shoulder. "Wow," he said, and for one quick moment, I was afraid he could read it.

But then I realized it was the Portuguese filling line after line that impressed him.

I shook my head when he reached for it, but did it in a friendly way. Instead, I folded it into quarters and put it carefully in my math book.

27

THE TRAINING TRACK

Another dinner, and again we hardly spoke; there was only the clink of knives and forks against the plates. Rafael did try, talking about a new horse Mrs. Januário had bought, and an exercise boy who would begin work next week.

I barely listened. I was thinking of arguments I'd had with Tio in Jales. He would stamp both feet, pulling at his mustache until he winced. I would yell, my voice as loud as his, and once I threw a book at the wall. Even Titia Luisa would slam the drawers in the kitchen so hard that everything in the house seemed to vibrate.

I remember how satisfying it all was, because after it was over, we'd sit in the three chairs on the porch, rocking, and one of us would start to laugh, setting the other two off.

But not here. Here was silence.

Echoing in my mind was Mamãe's voice: *You'll make a family.*

I hadn't done that, not even close.

But never mind that. There was something else I wanted to do. Would I dare? Yes, because the Horseman would do nothing, say nothing, no matter what I did.

I set my clock for four thirty the next morning so I'd be out of the house before Pai and Rafael were awake. I wanted to be in the barn before five, when they'd begin to exercise the horses.

But I didn't even need the alarm. I was wide awake by the time it rang. I threw on my clothes and went down to the kitchen to grab a banana out of the bowl, and another roll of peppermints from the drawer.

I was out of the house long before five. It was chilly, so I dipped my chin deep into my jacket.

José and an exercise boy were out on the track already, but a sliver of a girl was opening Wild Girl's stall, ready to exercise her. She grinned at me. "I'm Sara," she said in my own Portuguese. "I work here with the horses. Haven't seen you."

I nodded. "My father—" I began, and broke off.

"Our boss," she said. "He's a wonderful trainer. How well he knows horses!"

I broke in, barely breathing, trying to sound calm. "I'll be working with Wild Girl this morning. You want to exercise Love You instead?"

She shrugged. "Sure," she said, and moved down the aisle toward the end stall. I didn't look after her. I went inside, leaning against the wall to catch my breath. Then I realized I didn't even have the saddle.

I poked my head out the stall door, but the girl was gone, and no one else was paying attention to me. I went into the tack room, brought out what I needed to ride, and was back a moment later.

I reached for the peppermints in my pocket and fed one to Wild Girl and one to myself. "Remember me?" I asked her, touching that soft muzzle. "The girl with the candy?"

I put another peppermint on the ledge, and she reached for it. I buckled on a helmet, then saddled her, my hands remembering doing this so many times in Jales.

"A good taste, right?" I whispered. "I have more, and I can get tons of them. What do you say? Friends?"

She chewed with thick teeth, then curled her large tongue over them, watching me.

I reached out to her, raising my hand to run it over her neck, her silky skin rippling under my fingers. I leaned my head against her. "I haven't ridden in so long," I said. "Let me ride you. Let me pretend that you're Cavalo and we're home in Jales and heading across the field."

I pushed the stall door open with one hand and held the lead with the other. We walked along the aisle toward the high, open double doors in the back.

Wild Girl's head went up as she sniffed the outside air, and I smelled it, too. Spring! A slight mist was rising above the ground in wisps, and the overhead lights were still on. I could hear the faintest sound of music coming from the barn, and the clump of hooves on the oval. I pushed open the gate with my foot and clutched her black mane. Wild Girl never moved. She stood there quietly, her ears forward as if she was curious about me. She must have heard the sound of my breath, as I heard hers. . . .

Then I was up in the saddle, the fingers of one hand twisted in her wonderful wiry mane for a moment. I clicked my teeth, and it was as if we'd done this before, as if we'd done it a hundred times.

Three horses were up ahead, and I could just about see the girl on Love You.

Wild Girl started slowly along the track, and I let her lead me, let her decide. She came to a stop and looked around, almost as if we were in a field and not on that oval track.

She began to move. "How fast do you want to go?" I asked. "I won't hold you back."

Then she was galloping . . .

And by the turn, we were flying.

She was faster than Cavalo had ever been, faster than I could imagine. The wind was in my face, against my chest, my arms. The mist bathed my eyes, my cheeks.

She passed the other horses easily but slowed up behind Love You, letting the old mare lead before she began to race again. Something flitted through my mind, but it was gone in a moment because I was shouting to the wind, "I love you, Wild Girl, love you, love you. . . ."

This horse was mine, and as long as I had her to ride, I was home.

I turned my head slightly, glancing toward the fence. Pai

stood there, his hands on his hips, but we were going fast enough that I couldn't get a clear look at his face.

But I could imagine what he was thinking.

It was too bad I couldn't jump the fence with Wild Girl and just keep going.

Keep going forever.

28

THE BARN

Running.

Sweat cooling her back, her sides, sweat on her muzzle, a good feeling.

Water cascading over her, cleaning her, cooling her further.

The creature with the food, with the soft voice, in front of her.

But something else.

Something she had looked for all this time.

A mare.

A mare with a long tail running just in front of her.

A memory.

29

THE BEACH

Pai stood there, hands on his hips, watching me as I washed down Wild Girl. Instead of looking back at him, I tried to concentrate on the soapy rivers that ran down the horse's sides and legs.

Around us the barn was alive: pails were banging, José was turning up forkfuls of fresh-smelling hay, and Rafael was singing. I tried to concentrate on those noises, tried to keep my head close to Wild Girl.

I had about ten minutes to get out of there and get to school on time. How was I going to do that?

Quickly I rubbed Wild Girl down with soft dry cloths; I made sure there was plenty of mash in her pail. I felt a quick burst of happiness, thinking about our ride: a fast ride on a horse I loved, a horse that, like me, had come from far away.

I wasn't one bit sorry about what I had done, no matter what Pai would say.

I reached for my backpack, grabbed my jacket off the hook, and hesitated. There was something I should have remembered about that run. What was it?

But Pai blocked my way.

"I have to go to school," I said.

"Maybe you could miss this one day."

I looked at him, shocked, then nodded uncertainly. I followed him around the side of the house toward the truck. The big house was in front of us, and Mrs. Januário had opened her window. "Great ride," she called, waving down at me.

Pai muttered something under his breath, then opened the truck door. We pulled out onto the avenue, both of us silent. I was determined not to talk, but I was so curious about where we were going, it was hard not to ask.

Then he spoke. "Meadowbrook Parkway will take us to Jones Beach."

"A beach?" I said, in spite of myself. "It's only spring."

"Ai." He glanced at me. "You're just like my brother, Paulo."

I sputtered. "Look to yourself."

"We're all alike." He smiled a little. "But that's not such a bad thing."

I shook my head. He was wrong, of course. I wasn't a bit like either of them. Again we were silent. I found my fingers going to my upper lip, a thing Pai and Tio did. I pulled my hand away and leaned my forehead against the window.

Marshes stretched out on each side of us now, their beige

and gray somehow soothing. Birds flew up, one after another, dark against the sky. And in the distance was a water tower, tall and pointed, that appeared and disappeared as the truck curved around the parkway.

Then, spread out before us, was the sand, a carpet leading to water that stretched out forever. Waves curled over on themselves, sending geysers of spray into the air.

"The ocean," I whispered.

Pai nodded; then he parked the truck. We walked toward the water on sand that blew up miniature whirlwinds in front of us.

Seagulls followed, heads back, beaks open, screeching. I pictured Mamãe walking with us, her long hair blowing away from her face.

The Horseman pointed, and we went up on a boardwalk to tables in front of a cafeteria. "We'll have clam chowder," he said, "a warm soup on this cool day."

I sat on a bench out of the wind and waited while he went inside to get the soup, my face in the sun, listening to the crash of the waves. I couldn't get enough of the sea.

When the soup came, I couldn't get enough of that, either. It was hot and salty, and I felt it going all the way down.

"I have so much to say to you, Lidie," the Horseman said after a while.

Was he going to send me back to Jales? Now that I didn't want to leave Rafael, or school, or Wild Girl?

I glanced at him out of the corner of my eye. Did I want to leave *him*?

"Maybe we'll begin with Paulo," the Horseman said.

"Paulo?"

He reached into his pocket for a folded paper. "This letter came the other day; usually we just e-mail, a quick bit of this or that. Most of it is about horses, and the track, but this part is about you."

I took the letter from him, and he leaned over, his finger running along the words he wanted me to see: "She looks like her mother, but she acts like us. Have you seen her ride yet? She rides like no one I've ever seen. She's tough and strong, that girl, and as difficult as we are. I miss her. I wish I could be the one to show her the sea."

Now I was crying. Crying again. What was the matter with me? And the shock of it, seeing that Pai had tears in his eyes, too.

"Paulo was right," he said, and I waited for him to say *You were born to ride*. But instead, he sighed. "You *are* difficult."

I blurted out, "I'm not the difficult one."

"Really? You paid no attention to the room Rafael took days to paint. You ran away from school. You brought in a miserable stray cat that managed to spook a horse and cause an uproar in the barn. And this morning, without asking—"

"I—I don't pay attention to my brother?" I cut in, stuttering a little. "He's going through a terrible time. He's too big to ride. Do you know that? Did you help him with that? He's so worried—" I broke off; I'd said more than Rafael would have wanted me to say.

I took a breath. "There's no talking in our house, no dogs

134

barking, no cats, no birds singing, no laughing. . . ." I couldn't look at him. "There's nothing but silence in that house." I frowned. "Except for Rafael."

He nodded slowly. "That's true; I find it hard to say what's on my mind. But Rafael . . ."

"Yes, Rafael," I said.

He sighed. "I've been waiting for him to discover what he wants to do with himself. It can't be riding, I know that. But there are so many things he might do. There's his painting. Have you noticed the painting in the living room, the one in the hall . . .?"

So Rafael *had* painted them. "Beautiful."

"Maybe that will be what he'll do," Pai said, "but I don't think so. He's a fine student. I think he'll go to college, and become a veterinarian."

Where did that come from? Then I remembered Rafael out on the track taking care of Storm Cloud after that spill. I nodded. "Yes, I can see that."

Pai nodded. "But he's the one who has to see it."

My tears had stopped, but they were still as salty on my lips as the chowder. I tore open a pack of small crackers that had come with the soup and began to throw them, one by one, to a circle of hungry seagulls on the boardwalk.

Before I could think further, I felt his hand over mine. "Do you think I wanted to leave you? Rafael was older. I was taking him to an apartment that had one room. I had almost no money. . . ."

Two seagulls swooped down in front of me, and then two more.

"In a few minutes you'll have an army of gulls waiting to be fed." He pushed his pack of crackers toward me.

I opened the bag with my teeth. In front of me was a speckled gull with a curved yellow beak. I tossed the first cracker to him.

"When Mrs. Januário asked me to be her trainer, I knew a house went with it. I knew I could send for you," he said. "Rafael and I stood in front of that house, arms around each other. 'Lidie,' we said at the same moment. It was what we longed for all these years."

Salt was on my tongue, on my lips. I wasn't sure if it was from the crackers, or my tears, or the sea air.

"Before this, I saved, training horses, working early, working late, and Rafael, too. He went to school and exercised horses part-time. We managed to buy Doce, then every cent went into the bank so we could bring you here. There wasn't even enough money to go back to Jales more than once. But the house! It meant we could have you, and even buy the two horses."

Years of saving every cent, as I sat on the porch waiting. I heard the sound of my crying again over the birds; I felt his love for me for the first time since I came.

"About the horse," he said. "About Wild Girl. When I heard her name, when I heard she was for sale, I couldn't resist." He shook his head. "It's what Mamãe called you."

I looked at him now, this stern man whose face I suddenly recognized, my father, who had laughed as he held me up to the tree in the lemon grove.

Now the lemon seemed so unimportant, that he hadn't remembered it. But ah, Wild Girl.

He was still smiling, watching my face and nodding. "Ai, Paulo was right."

"Difficult," I said, smiling back.

"I never saw anyone ride like you."

I leaned into him as I threw the rest of the crackers to the gulls and wiped my eyes.

30

HOME

Pai was off looking at saddles at a tack shop, and Rafael was upstairs banging things around, whistling.

I was in the kitchen, longing for one of Titia Luisa's dinners, my mouth watering. At least, that was in the front of my mind. In back was what Pai was going to say when he found out what I'd done now.

I was humming anyway, doing some banging of my own. *Ai*, this kitchen!

In the refrigerator were only a few dark green leaves, four strips of bacon, and a pair of soft oranges. I'd used the last of the tuna fish an hour ago.

Rafael clumped downstairs again, out the kitchen door, and came back with a ladder.

"What are you doing?" I asked.

"Secret stuff. What are you doing?"

"Taking my turn for the cooking. About time, I guess."

"It depends on how well the meal turns out." He wiggled his eyebrows at me. "After all, Pai and I are gourmet cooks," he said as he went back upstairs.

I rattled through the cabinets and came up with a box of rice, a can of white beans, and another of stewed tomatoes. Holding one can in each hand, I weighed them in my mind.

You can make a meal out of anything, Titia Luisa would say. I thought of her clay *panelas*, those pots that she lined with rice and fresh cabbage and a dusting of spices. What could I do with these three things?

Then I had it.

In a little while, the tomatoes and beans were covered with bacon and bubbling in the oven. The rice was almost ready. The table was set, and the shredded salad greens and orange quarters, tossed in oil and vinegar, were in a bowl.

At six, I heard the front door open, and Pai came down the hall. Rafael was in back of him, his hands covered in what looked like putty or paint.

"Secret stuff," Rafael said again as he washed his hands at the sink.

We sat down to eat; the rice tasted like Titia Luisa's, and the invented bean recipe was fine. I watched as they both had seconds.

"Now," I said, and they both looked up. "You see I can cook."

"I see that," Pai said.

"So I will take my turn from now on."

"Do you think we'd argue about that?" Rafael said.

"So." I took the last forkful of beans, and they waited while I chewed.

"This is not a proper home," I told them. "Not the right kind of food."

They were looking at each other. "There's the fruit store, and the grocery," Rafael said. "Don't worry, we can—"

"But worse," I said, "the chairs in the living room are lined up so it seems we're waiting for the dentist to pull out our teeth."

"Is that why the living room door is closed today?" Rafael asked; then Pai said, "It's not so much of a thing to move the furniture."

I nodded. "There's more."

"*Ai,*" he said.

I pushed the salad bowl toward him. "I moved the horses in the stalls this afternoon. I put Wild Girl and Love You across from each other. They can look over their doors and say hello." I raised my shoulders. "Or whatever horses do."

"Whatever," Pai said, his finger on his upper lip. I could see he was hiding a smile.

"It didn't work with the cat, but I know Wild Girl needs a friend to make her happy."

"Like Billy, the pony who always traveled with Whirlaway," Rafael said.

"Exactly, yes," I said.

Pai piled the salad on his plate. "We do know a few things."

"I suppose that's what you were trying to do with the cat," Rafael said.

"But do you ever ask before you do anything?" Pai said.

"I'm asking now. . . ."

Pai tilted his head. "All right, it's fine."

"But I'm asking about something else." I hesitated, trying to think of how to say it. "In Jales, we had a canary, and a cat, and a dog." I spread my hands. "The bird sang in the kitchen, and sometimes the dog slept in my room."

Pai smiled a little. "You want a canary."

I took a breath and let it out. "I want a cat to begin with."

Pai's fingers went to his lip again. "What would we do with a cat?"

"I'll take care of her, feed her. A cat's not much work, you know."

"Why not?" Rafael said. "We can go down to the pet store. . . ."

I bit my lip. "She's in the living room, waiting."

Then we were laughing, and Pai, finished eating, stood up. On his way to put the dishes in the sink, he bent down and kissed the top of my head. "I'm glad you're here," he said gruffly.

Rafael piled my dishes up with his. "A family," he said.

Pai laughed. "With a difficult girl, and who knows what will be next!"

In the living room, I scooped up the orange cat from the puffiest chair. Already she'd left a few marks with all those claws. I put her face up to mine. She smelled a little like the tuna fish I'd given her. "Her name is Whirlaway," I called back to the kitchen.

I carried her up to my bedroom and nearly fell over the ladder in the doorway. Inside, the walls were coral, the color of the shirt I'd worn the day I'd come. The Minnie Mouse rug was gone.

"Don't ask me where the rug went," Rafael said, coming up the stairs.

Opposite my bed, Snow White and her dwarfs were hidden behind tissue-paper sketches. "I'll transfer them to the wall later," he said.

"Oh, Rafael." I hugged the cat and leaned forward to see what he'd drawn. There was a field of horses with their riders. At the very end was the blur of the starting gate, and beyond that a mass of carnations.

One horse with her jockey had paused to look at the carnations.

"Will she win the race?"

"Certainly."

"And the rider?" I asked.

"Ai, what do you think, Lidie?"

I knew it would be me.

"Perfect," I breathed.

At my desk, I sat answering the questions in my math book, the cat curled up beside me, as Rafael began to work on the wall.

I found the essay I'd written and ripped it into tiny pieces, watching Whirlaway dart after them. There was nothing left to wish for.

31

HOME

The hay in the filly's stall was fresh and piled up around the edges; it had the smell of a field. She raised one hoof and then the other, enjoying the feel of it underneath her.

She'd eaten, the warm mash steaming, and had her fill of cool water.

She was tired now after her long run, but still she put her head out the half door, curious to see what was happening outside.

Everything was quiet, the light dim, a creature asleep near the door. Across from her was the mare, watching her, ears pricked forward.

The mare whinnied, a soft sound, a good sound.

The filly whinnied back, contented, and then she slept.

ROME

ACKNOWLEDGMENTS

First, a thank-you to my husband, Jim, for the times we spent at Belmont and Aqueduct, sunny days, happy days, with memories of that first opening day so long ago, when I began to learn about the races.

Then, to my dear students at Clara H. Carlson, who told me more about Belmont—the cats, the chickens, that world that was just a short distance from the school.

This book was in my mind from the time I first learned about the beautiful silks made by Antoinette Brocklebank. Every time I saw a race, those colors captured me, and I knew they belonged in a book.

I owe a tremendous debt to Sheri Wilcox, who read this so carefully and gave me ideas, and to her father, Joseph Brocklebank, whose idea of Rafael's race was so much better than my own, of course. I hope I haven't disappointed them; any errors certainly are my own.

I can't forget my children, Jim and Laura, Bill and Cathie, Alice and Jim: my advisors, and critics, who give me joy. Their children, Jim, Chris, Bill, Cait, Conor, Patti, and Jilli, inspire me. I write for them.

PATRICIA REILLY GIFF is the author of many beloved books for children, including the Kids of the Polk Street School books, the Friends and Amigos books, and the Polka Dot Private Eye books. Several of her novels for older readers have been chosen as ALA-ALSC Notable Books and ALA-YALSA Best Books for Young Adults. They include *The Gift of the Pirate Queen; All the Way Home; Water Street; Nory Ryan's Song,* a Society of Children's Book Writers and Illustrators Golden Kite Honor Book for Fiction; and the Newbery Honor Books *Lily's Crossing* and *Pictures of Hollis Woods. Lily's Crossing* was also chosen as a *Boston Globe–Horn Book* Honor Book. Her most recent book was *Eleven.* Patricia Reilly Giff lives in Connecticut.